THE POKER BOY UNIVERSE

POKER BOY

The Slots of Saturn: A Poker Boy Novel

They're Back: A Poker Boy Short Novel

That Lost Riddle & Other Poker Boy Stories

The Portal of Wrong Love & Other Poker Boy Stories

The Secrets of Yesterday & Other Poker Boy Stories

You Forgive the Night's Scream & Other Poker Boy Stories

GHOST OF A CHANCE

The Poker Chip: A Ghost of a Chance Novel

The Christmas Gift: A Ghost of a Chance Novel

The Free Meal: A Ghost of a Chance Novel

The Cop Car: A Ghost of a Chance Novella

The Deep Sunset: A Ghost of a Chance Novel

MARBLE GRANT

THUNDER MOUNTAIN

Green Valley

SEEDERS UNIVERSE

Dust and Kisses: A Seeders Universe Prequel Novel

Against Time

Sector Justice

Morning Song

The High Edge

Star Mist

Star Rain

Star Fall

Starburst

Rescue Two

COLD POKER GANG

Kill Game

Cold Call

Calling Dead

Bad Beat

Dead Hand

Freezeout

Ace High

Burn Card

Heads Up

Ring Game

Bottom Pair

The Portal of Wrong Love & Other Poker Boy Stories

Dean Wesley Smith

WMG PUBLISHING

Contents

SNEAK PEEK
BEING DEAD (THE FIRST YEAR)

INTRODUCTION

Sometimes I have been known to just write "sweet" Poker Boy stories and the title story of this collection is one of those. Shows some history of some gods, but mostly the story is just sweet and fun.

In this collection, there are also a lot of poker games in the stories. Not sure why it worked out that way, but after all the hero is named Poker Boy and he is supposed to be the best poker player in the world. So poker games themselves are going to be involved.

I tried to keep them interesting. Honest.

And in this volume there is a cat story that introduces a brand new character named Pakhet Jones that I have now written numbers of novels and stories about. She is a superhero of cats. What writer can resist writing about cats?

Turns out the Poker Boy universe is huge. He helps out

Sky Tate at times. She is a superhero of detectives. And he is the landlord of two ghost agents, Marble Grant and Sims.

So expect brand new books in the future of brand new Poker Boy stories. And of his team. He has a lot more adventures in his future.

Hope you enjoy the stories.

DEAN WESLEY SMITH
LAS VEGAS, NEVADA

The Portal of Wrong Love & Other Poker Boy Stories

The Portal Of Wrong Love

Chapter One

When your girlfriend appears and tells you that there may be a problem, any sane man perks up and pays attention.

Close attention.

I'm Poker Boy, a superhero in the poker universe, and my girlfriend, Patty Ledgerwood, aka Front Desk Girl, is also a superhero. So not only could a "problem" be in our relationship, but it could be something that meant the world was about to explode, and we had ten minutes to save everyone or die trying.

Yeah, that saving the world thing has happened a few times. Honest.

So when she appeared and said that there may be a problem, it was sort of a double "pay attention" moment.

Patty still wore her white blouse, brown slacks, and brown vest from her front desk job at the MGM Grand.

I'd just finished playing in a poker tournament down at the Golden Nugget, so I was still in my black leather coat, fedora-like hat, and jeans that; is my superhero costume for the most part.

I hadn't expected Patty to get off work for a few more hours, at least. So I'd gotten some fries and a vanilla milkshake, and was sitting in the big diner booth in my office, just eating and staring out over the city, enjoying the moment of quiet.

Superheroes don't get many moments of quiet, and, if I'd realized that, I would have also realized the moment was about to end.

"We got a problem," Patty said, appearing beside the booth and sliding in next to me and taking a fry.

I did the right thing and perked up, paid attention, focused on her, and asked, "Good problem, bad problem, world-ending problem?"

Granted, not the smartest thing for a boyfriend to say, but she had caught me by surprise.

"I don't honestly know," Patty said, munching her fry and looking worried. "Never seen anything like this before."

She took another fry and motioned for me to follow her over to the window.

My office is an invisible glass cube that floats about a thousand feet in the air over The Las Vegas Strip. A few extra chairs and the old diner booth that sits in the very center of the room are the only furniture. I had put a wooden railing all the way around the inside of the glass to kill the feeling that any moment we might fall off the black-and-white tiled floor to our deaths on the hot pavement below.

Patty pointed to a woman on the street corner near the front of the MGM Grand main entrance. From this height, the woman looked to be in high heels, wearing a very short mini-skirt and a blouse. She had a big orange purse over her shoulder.

It was a hot September day out there, so that street corner must have been over a hundred degrees the way the sun radiated off all the concrete in this town.

A couple of our adventures had started with us looking down on the street below, but this sure didn't seem like an adventure, or even a problem. I was feeling no sense of worry or dread or anything, other than a desire to go back and finish my fries and milkshake.

We watched for a moment as a couple near the curb moved slightly to go around the woman. The couple seemed to be arguing, and not happy with each other in any fashion. The woman reached out and touched the man, sort of like she was handing him a flyer or something, but I didn't see anything in her hand.

Then, still arguing, the couple seemed to walk into an opening in the air and just—vanish.

"What the hell?" I said, blinking to see if I had actually seen what just happened.

Again, I had no sense at all of danger from the woman, no sense that any harm was coming to the people who vanished.

"So, you've never seen this before?" I asked Patty as we both watched the woman stand there, seeming to just be casually waiting, like a hooker on a street corner. Now that I looked a little closer, she sort of looked like a hooker, even though they were illegal in Las Vegas. Of course, that didn't stop them much.

"Never," Patty said. "But I'm not getting a sense of danger from any of this."

"Neither am I," I said. "But we got to figure this out. That couple had to have gone somewhere."

I glanced up at the ceiling, which I always did out of habit when calling my boss. "Stan, a little help?"

Stan, my boss and the God of Poker, arrived an instant later. Just as I always wore a black coat, a black fedora-like hat, and jeans, Stan always wore a 1960s-style button-down cardigan sweater, tan slacks, and tan loafers. His hair was cut short and he looked like he could sell insurance in 1965.

Patty pointed to the woman below. It took Stan a moment staring at the woman before he said, "Go to hell."

Then he vanished.

"God of Poker swearing is never a good sign," I said.

Patty only nodded. "Another couple is heading toward her. What should we do?"

"If we stop them, are we saving them?" I asked.

Patty shrugged. "Not a clue."

"If she's doing something nasty to them," I said, "we'll never live with ourselves if we don't stop her."

"True," Patty said. "Very true."

Chapter Two

I teleported us to a spot in front of the couple.

They both sort of jerked back and stopped as Patty and I appeared in front of them.

"Sorry for the surprise," I said, giving them my best smile as Patty sent calming emotions toward the two. "Sidewalk is closed for repair."

The couple, clearly from a part of the country where people didn't just materialize in front of them, stepped back, then they both turned and walked damned fast away from us.

Patty and I turned to face the woman.

I was right. The woman looked like a well-worn hooker, with a tight skirt far, far too short for her older legs. She had on a very thin white blouse that left little to the imagination, and what was under the blouse was not something I had ever wanted to imagine. Or see, for that matter.

She looked like a hooker, but one right out of central casting from a "B" movie, if the cast had come from a nursing home.

"So, where did you send that last couple?" I asked.

She smiled and my bet was that if it wasn't so hot, the caked-on makeup on her face would have cracked. Her teeth looked rotted and one was missing, and her smile didn't come close to reaching her eyes, what little I could see of them through all the makeup and wrinkles.

But even with all that, I still wasn't getting a sense of danger from her in the slightest.

"Front Desk Girl," she said. "Poker Boy, it is an honor to meet you both. I have heard so much about you."

Both Patty and I stayed a good four steps away from the woman, just standing there on the hot sidewalk. "Who do we have the pleasure of talking with?" I asked.

Stan and Laverne appeared beside us on the sidewalk at that moment and took all of us out of time, freezing the traffic around us.

Laverne, Lady Luck herself, was dressed in a gray pants suit with her long brown hair pulled back tight, giving her an even more severe look than normal.

I only wished that these time bubbles would also block out the heat, but they didn't, and my leather jacket and hat were quickly becoming too much for this hot sidewalk in early September.

"Ishtar," Laverne said, stepping forward slightly, but not going near the old woman. "It has been far too long."

I did my best to place the name. Clearly an old god of some sort, but all that was coming to me was the name of a bad movie.

"Oh, my," Patty said softly beside me.

I glanced at the love of my life. Patty's eyes were huge and she was just staring in almost shock at the old hooker.

I knew at that point I was in one of those moments where my youth and lack of knowledge of all the gods was putting me at a disadvantage. And when that happened, which seemed to be more than I wanted to admit—even to myself—I always figured silence was just the smartest thing I could do.

"Good to see you again, Laverne," Ishtar said to Lady Luck.

Neither woman bowed to the other, so I figured there was bad blood somewhere in the past between the two.

"Does Gil know you have left Uruk?" Laverne asked, her voice not cold, but not warm and welcoming and friendly either.

"That impotent fool couldn't find his ass with both hands," Ishtar said. "Just sits in his chair and rocks all day, smiling at who knows what. I needed to get back to work, have an adventure."

Laverne nodded and glanced at Stan, who instantly vanished.

"So, where were you sending the couples?" Laverne asked.

Ishtar laughed. Not a nice sound, more like fingernails across a blackboard. I am sure that if we weren't inside a time bubble at the moment, that laugh would have caused car wrecks on the busy street beside us.

"Ishtar?" Laverne said, her voice sounding more insistent.

"No damn fun," the old hooker said, seeming to pout under all the makeup. "I sent them through my portal of love to bed, of course. In that towering palace."

The old woman pointed to the MGM Grand.

I wanted to laugh at the image, but I didn't. More than likely those couples ended up naked in a bed in some strange room in the MGM Grand. That might be interesting to try to explain, especially if their clothes vanished along the way.

Patty said, "I'll get it covered."

Then she vanished.

"You understand, don't you, Laverne?" Ishtar said. "Life can be very boring and I just had to get out."

"This is a very different world now from old Babylonia," Laverne said. "Or Atlantis before that."

"I know, and I find it exciting," Ishtar said. "Just the new fashions, this thing called makeup. It is wonderful to behold, don't you agree?"

A moment later Stan appeared with a stately man. He was tall with powerful shoulders and a full head of gray hair. He was dressed in a long, white robe and wore sandals. He carried a long staff that he seemed to use for balance.

"Laverne," the man said, his voice deep and powerful. He bowed slightly to Lady Luck.

"Gil," Laverne said, bowing slightly in return.

The man named Gil turned to look at Ishtar, then shook his head and made a motion with one hand toward her.

Ishtar instantly changed from looking like an old hooker to a beautiful, but aging woman with clear skin and bright silver hair and perfect white teeth. She also wore a white flowing robe and sandals.

I was surprised at the change in her, from a low-level hooker to looking like a goddess in an instant.

"What a spoilsport," Ishtar said, looking down at how she was now dressed.

At that moment Patty appeared. "No one was transported into the hotel."

Laverne glanced back at Patty, suddenly worried.

She then turned back to Ishtar. "Is the portal you used still open?"

It is," Ishtar said, laughing, this time in a way that actually conveyed amusement. She pointed at a place in the sidewalk just beyond where she stood. "My special portal of love, as I like to call it."

"How many couples did you send through the portal, dear?" the man named Gil asked, clearly used to being patient with Ishtar.

I was starting to get the idea that Ishtar wasn't well. Laverne and Gil both treated her with respect, but also almost as a child.

"Six wonderful couples," Ishtar said. "They were not happy with each other, so I sent them to their beds of love in the magnificent tower."

Again she pointed to the MGM Grand.

Patty shook her head as Laverne again glanced at her.

Now, for the first time, my warning sense was starting to activate.

And activate big time.

Those couples were in trouble.

Chapter Three

Gil waved his hand at Ishtar, and she froze.

Then he turned to face Laverne and the rest of us. "In her state, there is no telling exactly where those couples ended up."

Laverne nodded. "Are her powers fading with her memory?"

"They are," Gil said. "And becoming erratic. It's tragic to watch, but I do my best to keep track of her. I'm sorry about this."

"We know you do your best for your love," Laverne said, her voice clearly sad.

Until this moment, it had never occurred to me that a god could get dementia. How horrible for anyone, human or god. Losing my mind was one of the things that scared me more than I wanted to ever admit.

I made myself take a deep breath of the hot air and glance at Patty, then back at Laverne and Gil, who were standing silently looking at each other.

"Any way to trace where that portal goes from this side?" I asked, breaking into their lost thoughts.

Both Laverne and Gil shook their heads.

"Those couples are lost somewhere," Laverne said. "There's just no telling where."

I glanced at Patty and smiled, giving her a one-eyebrow raise.

She laughed. "I was afraid you were thinking that."

I turned to Laverne and Gil and Stan. "I think you need to release Ishtar and let her send me and Patty through the portal as well."

"There is no telling," Gil said, looking very worried, "with her decreased abilities, where or when you might end up."

"When?" Patty asked, the worry clear in her voice.

Laverne nodded. "Ishtar had the ability to send lovers through time."

"We can't let those six couples be on their own," I said, forcing myself to not think about the real consequences of walking through a portal made by a woman not completely in control of her powers. "Especially if they are in the past. Remember the last time we left people from this time remain in the past? We need to return them to here and now. And the only way to find those couples is to follow them."

"I agree," Patty said.

Gil just shook his head in amusement. "Now I see how these two young superheroes got their reputation."

"I pretty much hate this idea," Stan said. "But darned if I can think of another one."

Laverne nodded and turned to Gil. "Release Ishtar and let's do this."

Gil nodded and waved his hand, and Ishtar smiled as if nothing had happened.

"We would like to go through your portal of love," I said, taking Patty's hand and stepping down the sidewalk toward her.

"Oh, wonderful," Ishtar said, her smile beaming. The portal is still open. Just walk this way."

She indicated we should walk past her.

As we walked in front of her, she reached out and touched me slightly, giving me a wonderful smile.

Then a step later, the heat and the Las Vegas Boulevard vanished.

And so did my clothes.

CHAPTER FOUR

atty and I ended up completely naked in a vast, rolling field of what looked like wildflowers of some sort.

All the flowers were blooming in a rainbow of colors, and white clouds drifted lazily through a bright blue sky. The temperature was warm, but not hot like it had been on the street in Las Vegas.

It felt perfect.

The flowers came up above our knees and the ground underneath felt soft and inviting. You could lie down in the flowers, and no one would see you twenty feet away.

"I don't think we're in Kansas anymore," I said, smiling at the wonderful woman I was in love with, who didn't seem to mind at all that she was standing naked in the middle of a field of beautiful flowers.

Damn she looked good.

I mean really, really good.

"These aren't poppies," Patty said. Then she waved her hand and we were dressed again just as we had been in Las Vegas. She was in her MGM Grand front desk uniform and I was back in my jeans, shirt, leather jacket and hat.

"Ah, bummer," I said. "I was enjoying the view."

""I'll give you a view later," Patty said, smiling at me. "Remember why we're here. And block the love potion part of this place."

At that moment I realized my warning senses were going off big time. She was right, there was clearly something in the air here.

I blocked out and contained all feelings of love and lust and so on, and suddenly felt almost myself again.

"That was strange," I said.

Patty nodded. "Figured from the view of the god of sex and love and prostitution, where she sent us would be filled with things to help out the cause."

"I don't remember us needing much help," I said, laughing.

She laughed as well. "Now focus. We need to find those other couples."

"First," I said, "let's see if we can figure out when and where we are."

Patty nodded and I glanced up and shouted, "Stan."

A moment later Stan, Laverne, the man named Gil, and Ishtar appeared.

I was very, very happy to see them.

Gil glanced around as Ishtar just sort of danced among the flowers.

"I should have guessed," Gil said. "Elysium. She loves this place. Always did, didn't you dear?"

"My favorite place," Ishtar said, continuing to just twirl and skip and dance like a kid in the flowers.

I was stunned to say the least. I had always assumed Elysium was in the underworld.

"Where exactly are we?" I asked, almost afraid of the answer.

"Denmark," Laverne said, matter-of-factly.

At that moment, a woman squealed and some flowers rustled about fifty paces away and a woman sat up. She was naked and clearly making love to a man under her in the flowers.

"Seems we found the missing couples," Gil said, smiling. "Or at least one couple."

"The others are here," Laverne said. "Similarly occupied."

"A wonderful place," Ishtar said, dancing in circles around them through the flowers.

"We'll come back regularly," Gil said, moving over to take Ishtar's hand.

"Oh, can we?" Ishtar asked like a kid being offered a trip to get ice cream.

"We can," Gil said, smiling.

Then he nodded and bowed slightly to Laverne, and Gil and Ishtar were gone.

"How long has she been like that?" I asked.

"Most of a century," Laverne said, her voice sad.

I had no idea what to think. I had never, ever thought of the downsides of living a very, very long time. Now losing my mind scared me even more than it did before.

At that moment, the woman in the flowers let out a high-pitched sigh of pleasure, fell forward, and vanished from sight.

Laverne turned to Patty. "I'll alert your boss at the MGM Grand that six rooms are going to be needed in a few minutes, and Stan will bring the room numbers back to you and help in the transport."

"We'll wait here and then get the couples to the rooms," I said, nodding. "And we'll leave them clothes for when they surface...or run out of energy."

Laverne nodded, and she and Stan vanished.

"An amazing place," Patty said, looking around at the vast rolling fields of flowers and the wonderful blue sky. "I've always heard about this place, never thought I would actually see it. It's more beautiful than I had ever imagined."

Behind them, laughter echoed over the flowers.

I took Patty's hand and turned as a naked couple jumped up and the woman chased the man about twenty feet through the field until she caught him. Then laughing, they again vanished from sight, tumbling into the soft flowers.

"Damn that looks like fun," I said, smiling at the woman I loved beside me.

Patty laughed. "It does, doesn't it? Tell you what? Later

tonight I'll chase you naked around my apartment a few times."

"Promise?" I asked.

"Promise," she said, squeezing my hand.

A sigh of pleasure echoed over the flowers from somewhere. And damned if I wasn't sure if it was me doing the sighing.

The Rude Improbable Presumptive

CHAPTER ONE

He called himself The Presumptive.

That might have been the most stupid nickname I have ever heard a guy call himself at a poker table.

But Idiot Boy (as I liked to call him, but not out loud) thought the name fit his poker playing, I guess making him the presumptive winner. Actually, from his poker game, his nickname should have been Long-Time Loser.

The game was a good one, a nice no-limit game at my home casino in the Oregon Mountains. Spirit Winds Casino was a small place in comparison to Vegas standards, yet friendly and welcoming.

I had jumped from my office in Las Vegas to the casino at 6 p.m. right after Patty had gone to work at the MGM Grand.

I had first checked on the progress of the luxury home we

were having built in the mountains a few miles from the casino, and then managed to get into the no-limit game around 7 p.m. as it started up.

Patty didn't get off work until two in the morning, so I was looking forward to a fun night of poker and making a little money.

The Spirit Winds poker room was a great place with fifteen tables, a friendly staff, and brushes and dealers who knew how to keep the games fun and relaxed. As with everything in the casino, the wood and brown tones helped make the place feel relaxed.

Televisions were tucked up against the ceiling all the way around the room, always playing sports events without sound, and the noise from the casino was a background noise, but not intrusive. So a player could actually hear a normal conversation at a table instead of having to shout as in some poker rooms.

This had always been my home casino, and even though I lived most of my time in Las Vegas, I loved being able to teleport to play here a few times a week. A completely different feeling than any Las Vegas poker room, that was for sure.

The Presumptive had to be no older than twenty-five, with dark short hair, black eyes, and almost white skin that he mostly kept hidden with long sleeves and a buttoned collar. From the looks of his rings, watch, and clothes, he had more money than he knew what to do with.

I had learned over the years that people with a lot of

money sometimes, but not always, had great egos and a sense of entitlement.

I had a lot of money, and at times a large ego, especially at a poker table, but no sense at all of entitlement. I had earned every bit of my money and there would have been a time a decade or more ago I would never have sat down in a game this rich.

Tonight, I figured The Presumptive was going to entitle me to a large percentage of his money.

He ended up sitting at the other end of the table from me so I could see him directly.

He was brash and loud, but also had a level of uncertainty that he tried to hide with his brashness. He had also made a really, really stupid mistake by buying in with far too many chips.

I had bought in for two thousand. He had come to the table with five times that much in racks of chips. I was going to enjoy walking away from the table later on with those chips in racks.

After twice around the table, I had played no hands, just tossed all my cards away. But that allowed me to watch and get a good read on him.

He played fast and loose and tried to intimidate with his large stack of chips. And actually, in the right situation, that was a decent way to play, but not right off as a game started.

His second major mistake.

About half the table was made up of regular players in the room, all solid players, and they just sat back and stayed out of the guy's way as I did. A couple young kids from the Portland area mixed it up with him on a few early hands and both dinged a small amount out of the guy's stack, which made The Presumptive play even more aggressive.

The way to fight an overly aggressive player like him was to sit back and wait for a great hand and then play it weak and let him bet and then take his chips.

One hour into the game, I started to get a different read on Idiot Boy. He had started to become worried as he got down to about half his chips left in his stack.

I could sense the worry like it was a bad odor of a disease.

I knew that odor. It was addictive gambling odor and I had seen it more times than I ever wanted to think about on people in casinos.

And the more worried he got, the brasher he became, almost rude, and his play got more aggressive, which made his chips drop even faster.

When his chips got down to only two thousand left, he stood and moved to the cage and bought in for another ten thousand chips.

That was when it dawned on me that he might not be actually playing on his own money, but had set up a line-of-credit with the casino. In other words, he had good credit and was playing with borrowed money.

A horrid thing to do and the way he got more worried, the credit might have been a sham of some sort or another.

After another hour, he was down another six thousand, about three of it sitting in front of me.

And numbers of tourists had cycled through the game, leaving their money before they left. All the regulars were just smiling because they had stumbled into a game made in heaven.

But The Presumptive almost stank from worry and addiction. To everyone else he kept it covered with brashness and sometimes just flat rudeness.

I needed to find out what was really going on.

Chapter Two

I waited until the attention was distracted to the other end of the table and then froze time around me.

Actually, I didn't stop time, I just stepped between moments of time, but it had the appearance that I had frozen time.

Then I stood and said toward the ceiling, "Stan, need a little help."

Stan, my boss, the God of Poker, appeared a moment later.

He was dressed as he always dressed, in a button down sweater, tan slacks, and brown loafers. With his plain face and short brown hair, he was the most nondescript person I had ever met. He liked to stay hidden.

On the other hand, I liked to be right out there. I always

wore a black leather coat and a fedora-like black hat. I called it my superhero uniform.

When Stan appeared, I indicated the guy at the end. "Know him? He calls himself "The Presumptive."

Stan glanced at my large stacks of winnings and then laughed. "You must be in heaven playing with him."

"So never seen or heard of him before?" I asked.

Stan just looked at the guy a little more without answering. "He's playing scared. More than likely on borrowed money, even though he pretends to be rich with those rings and such. He's got an addiction problem."

Wow, my boss was good. No wonder he was the God of Poker. He could read a guy at a glance.

"My take on him exactly," I said. "This is a small casino and he might be getting this money on credit. I don't know, but he shows no signs of slowing down giving his money away."

"Think he's pulling a scam of some sort or another?" Stan asked.

"Can't figure it out though, whatever it is. Might just be a rich kid playing with parents' money, but I don't think so. I'm getting a sense of something more."

Stan nodded. "He might have just expected to win and sat down at the exact wrong table."

"He called himself The Presumptive so very possible," I said.

Stan stared at the guy for a moment, then asked, "Second buy in?"

"Second," I said. "Ten thousand both times."

Stan nodded and smiled at me like a parent looking at a child. "He will make three more rebuys, all ten grand. Take his money and let me know when you get it figured out. But don't let him leave the casino without calling me."

With that Stan vanished.

I was sure I could hear him laughing as I went back to my chair and got back into the flow of time.

Stan knew what was happening and he wanted me to figure it out.

How annoying.

Almost as annoying as Idiot Boy at the other end of the table.

Not quite, but close.

Chapter Three

So much for my pleasurable game at my home casino while Patty worked. I focused in even more on both playing great cards and watching for any idea of what Idiot Boy was up to.

When he got down to two thousand in chips again, he went and rebought another ten thousand.

I now had a good nine thousand in front of me and the other four regulars who knew how to play against Idiot Boy's type of play had thousands each as well.

We were just plucking this guy like a dead chicken.

And his smell of fear and addiction just seemed to increase. I was amazed that no one around me could even smell it.

Finally, as he rebought for his fifth time, I couldn't take it any longer. If he was borrowing this money and planning on a scam, he was going to hit this casino for fifty thousand and that was too much.

I froze time again and jumped into the financial cage, something I almost never did.

They had his tab right on the counter clear as day. He had put fifty thousand in cash on deposit. He wasn't scamming the casino or playing on credit. It was his money and he had gone through it all, except for the chips in front of him on the table.

I jumped back to the table and let myself back into the flow of time.

With his last ten thousand on the table, I decided to try to engage him a little in conversation.

After he lost a fairly large pot to one of the regulars that Idiot Boy had kept raising over and over, I said to him. "Tough night, huh?"

He looked at me and shook his head. "My lot in life."

My little voice screamed at that answer. It wasn't the answer of a man fearful of losing, but a person resigned to his place.

"Looks like you can afford the loss," I said. "We all have them."

"I always have them," he said. "I'll go back, get more money, and then lose it again."

"So the nickname?" I asked as he shoved in his last two thousand in chips to cover a bet.

I was starting to understand. His nickname wasn't that he was the presumptive winner, but the presumptive loser.

"Just a joke for myself," he said, shaking his head.

"What's the punishment for?" I asked. "What did you do?"

As his last bit of money was pushed to another player, he looked at me and I think, for the first time, he finally saw me. He had been under some sort of screen to not be able to see me before he lost all his money.

And that screen had kept me from seeing him clearly as well. He now radiated power equal to that of a god.

A very old and powerful god.

Holy smokes, what had I just done?

He smiled at me and then shook his head. Then he looked up at the ceiling, all smell of worry and fear gone completely.

"Really?" he asked to the ceiling. "I mean, really?"

I took us both out of time and it didn't even startle him.

"Stan?" I said into the air. "We're done."

Stan appeared next to Laverne, Lady Luck herself. This guy really, really must be on the shit list if Laverne was here.

Laverne looked her normal stern self with a pinstriped business suit on and her hair pulled back tight off her face.

The guy stood up and joined the three of us standing near my end of the table.

"You going to be all right, Hermes?" Laverne asked, her face actually showing some compassion.

"Feeling fine again," he said, moving his shoulders around. "This treatment really works. Thanks."

The guy I had been silently calling Idiot Boy turned and shook my hand. "Glad I can remember that game," he said.

"It was a pleasure playing with Poker Boy. I've heard so much about you. And you being able to spot me is really amazing."

I was just standing there feeling shocked. I had played a night of poker with one of the original gods of gambling, Hermes.

And kicked his ass.

And he wasn't angry.

Kicking a god's ass often resulted in great anger that resulted in earthquakes and lightning and all sorts of other really nasty stuff.

But for Hermes, the losing had clearly been a treatment of some sort.

"Thank you," I said. "But you had me worried."

Hermes nodded. "Yeah, this is sort of all my gambling addictions wrapped into one evening every five years or so. But by doing this, lancing the wound, so to speak, I don't need to gamble for another five years. A night like this just cleans me out."

"Makes Sally happy," Laverne said, smiling.

"That it does," Hermes said, laughing. "And never hurts to have the wife happy."

Clearly this Hermes was liked in his real, unprotected form.

At that moment, Patty appeared next to me. I hadn't realized how long the evening had taken and she was already off work and dressed in a casual blouse and jeans.

When she saw Stan and Laverne, she smiled and then turned to Hermes. "How have you been? How's Sally?"

My girlfriend knew Hermes. Holy smokes!

"She's doing great and going to be waiting for me to get home with a bottle of nice wine and a good dinner," Hermes said. "Thanks to your boyfriend here, I'm going to be early."

"Yeah," Patty said, laughing, "he can cause people to leave a poker table quickly."

"Not sure how to take that," I said.

Patty kissed my cheek. "In the best possible way."

And I had no idea how to take that, or the fact that everyone was laughing.

Hermes just patted my shoulder. "Poker Boy, you can help me with my treatment any time you want."

"Thanks," I said. "But I had no idea that you would be here tonight."

"So this was just happenstance?" he asked, shaking his head.

Hermes glanced back at all the stacks of chips in front of my position at the table and the stacks in front of the other regulars who had ridden this right down with me. "Certainly helps me understand that there are a lot better players in the world than I am. I think once every five years is enough."

With that he kissed Laverne's cheek, shook Stan's hand, hugged Patty, then shook my hand. "Let's get this back into real time so I can get out of here. I got dinner waiting."

"And you have a girlfriend waiting," Patty said to me, smiling. "I'll be home."

With that Patty and Laverne and Stan vanished.

As Hermes walked back to his seat, he laughed. "Looks to me, Poker Boy, that tonight, we are both winners."

I nodded. "In a far more important game than is played at this table."

"Got that right," Hermes said, smiling at me. "Totally right."

THE LIBRARY OF ATLANTIS

Chapter One

"There is a god of the Internet?" I asked, knowing instantly that my blurted out question was flat stupid. Of course there was, there was a god for everything that existed it seemed.

Stan, the God of Poker and my direct boss, just gave me the look he always gives me when I have asked a question beyond my normal stupid. Then he shook his head. He had on his usual gray sweater vest, gray slacks and open shirt, also a non-color. Stan was the dullest dresser I had ever met and he never altered what he wore.

Of course, I wasn't much better considering I only wore jeans, a dress shirt, a black leather coat and a fedora-like hat. I considered the coat and hat my superpower costume. Stan shook his head every time I mentioned that as well.

Patty, aka Front Desk Girl and my girlfriend, patted my

leg and laughed lightly. She had her long brown hair pulled back and had on a wonderful white blouse and tan slacks. She had added color to the outfit with a turquoise necklace and earrings. When she patted my leg like that, I knew the question was beyond stupid.

I started to ask who it was, then just shut my mouth and decided one foot in my mouth at a time was enough, especially right before lunch on a warm summer's day.

The three of us were sitting in the large diner booth in the center of my office. My office was invisible and floated about a thousand feet above the Las Vegas strip. It had four glass walls, which made the view of the desert and subdivisions and mountains surrounding Las Vegas just stunning. And at night, the lights of the city were fantastic.

Patty and I liked to come up here at times and just sit with our feet up on the wood railing around the entire office and stare out at the stars above and the lights below. Just saying, that view had started many a romantic evening.

Besides a few chairs, the only furniture in the square room was a replica of a diner's booth with a tan Formica tabletop and a red vinyl bench seat that wrapped around three sides. At the moment, Patty and I were sharing a vanilla milkshake in a tall glass and Stan was working all by himself on a massive chocolate milkshake that he seemed to be studying more than drinking.

Madge would be bringing us lunch shortly. She was a superhero in food service and owned the diner in downtown Vegas where my team used to meet. When this office was built, we put in a connection to the diner from this office that she uses to bring us food and drinks. And team members without teleporting powers use that entrance as well.

Madge liked having us up here in this office better than in her restaurant, since we didn't clog up a booth for regular customers and didn't spook people by teleporting in and out all the time. She said it had been like expanding her restaurant by one table without all the costs and construction problems.

Suddenly Ben appeared in front of the table. Ben was the oldest-looking god I had ever met and looked like anyone's short, balding grandfather, right down to the too-large suit jacket and pants that didn't match. His brown leather shoes looked like he had bought them a hundred years ago and never even dusted them off.

He had been the God of Lamplighters, but as that profession faded, Stan and I saved him, got him to join my team and also got him a new job as one of the Gods of Books and Libraries.

I considered Ben our brains. Because his job for centuries had been so dull, he had been an avid reader of every text he could find, and he could remember everything, and I do mean everything, no matter how many centuries ago he had read it.

"Join us," Patty said, smiling at Ben and motioning for me to scoot over which I did. Lunch in my office often turned into a team affair and I honestly liked that.

Ben shook his head. "Got a problem."

At that, Stan seemed to come back into his eyes and

pointed to the open spot beside Patty. "Sit and tell us about it."

Ben nodded. Then as he slid in, he said, "Maybe I should tell Laverne at the same time."

At that point my warning bells were going off in full seven-alarm mode in the back of my mind. Laverne was one of the most powerful gods in the world. She was also known by the name Lady Luck.

"Laverne?" Stan said into the air, slight worry creeping into his eyes. Stan had a perfect poker face. Me being able to see worry on it just made my alarm bells ring louder.

Patty touched my leg and I calmed some. She had the wonderful gift of being able to keep me calm through just about anything. I loved that superpower of hers.

"Right here," Laverne said, appearing and pulling over a chair so she could sit at the end of the table. She had on her standard gray silk business suit. Her hair was pulled back tight giving her thin face a stark look and the entire outfit made her seem even more powerful than she was, if that was possible.

She turned to Ben. "So what's the problem?"

"The Library of Atlantis," he said, looking distraught.

Stan sat forward, clearly worried.

Laverne did the same.

I wanted to ask how Atlantis could have a library since the entire continent sunk a whole bunch of centuries ago, but decided now was not the time for my second really dumb question of the day.

"Is there something wrong at the library?" Laverne asked.

Ben nodded. "Very wrong."

If I didn't know better, I would have sworn old Ben was about to burst into tears. He normally was the coolest, the calmest of anyone on my team.

We all stayed silent until Ben took a deep breath, gathered himself, and looked directly at Laverne.

"A book is missing."

Now, if this had been April 1st, I would have fallen out of the booth laughing. And luckily for me, I didn't even snort because Patty, Stan, and Laverne were acting as if this really was the end of the world as they knew it.

"How is that possible?" Laverne asked.

"I don't know," Ben said. "None of us do. It just isn't possible, yet it happened."

"It can't happen," Laverne said, her voice almost angry.

When Lady Luck got angry, you didn't want to be anywhere around.

"We know that," Ben said. "But it did happen and that's why I came here. We searched everywhere. This is a last resort before the entire fabric of everything we know starts to unravel."

Unravel?

Fabric of everything?

Now he had my attention.

CHAPTER TWO

I sat there silently, something fairly unusual for me, as Laverne and Stan peppered Ben with questions about what he and the other Gods of Books and Libraries and all the superhero librarians working for them had done to find this missing book.

It seems they had looked everywhere. They had searched all recently filed books in case the missing book had been misfiled.

Then they had done the unthinkable to Ben. They had run an entire inventory of the entire library, physically checking to make sure every book was in place with no extra book anywhere.

It seemed the book had left the library and that was a very, very, very bad thing for reasons I had yet to figure out.

Finally Laverne stood. "We need to go to the Fates."

With that, she and Ben were gone.

"We are so screwed," Stan said, going back to staring at his milkshake.

At that point Madge came in carrying our lunch. She had on her typical too-tight pink uniform with a white apron that I swore had stains on it from the last century. And she always wore far, far too much makeup for any human face.

She looked around and frowned which managed to not crack her makeup. "I thought Ben and Laverne were here as well."

"They were," Patty said. "They had to go. There is a problem at the Library of Atlantis."

Madge set a wonderful-smelling cheeseburger in front of me nestled on a basket of fries. She gave Patty her club sandwich, and then Stan his cheeseburger. She might look the part of a back-road waitress gone to seed, but she was the best short-order cook I had ever had the pleasure to meet.

"So what's the problem at the library?" she asked.

"A book is missing," Stan said, his voice low.

Madge sort of froze in mid-step. Then she looked back at Stan.

"You are kidding, right?"

"Nope," Stan said.

"We are so screwed," Madge said, heading for the entrance to the diner.

That was enough for me. I needed some answers and I needed them fast, no matter how stupid my questions sounded.

"Stan, could you jump and tell Screamer we are having an emergency meeting. Have him bring Sherrie."

He nodded and vanished.

I turned to Patty. "I'm going to need to ask more than my normal number of really stupid questions here very soon if we're going to help with this. Stick with me, all right?'

She nodded.

At that moment Stan came back. A moment later Screamer and Sherrie appeared.

Screamer was about my height at six foot and wore jeans and a dress shirt and a light sports jacket. He normally worked for the police because his main superpower was the ability to get into people's minds with a touch.

Sherrie was Screamer's wife and worked as a superhero for food and beverage tending bar in Reno. She was also one of Lady Luck's four daughters. Today she had on a short black skirt, a white blouse, and an apron with the name of a casino on it. Clearly she had been at work.

"So what's emergency," Screamer asked as Stan let him and Sherrie scoot into the booth and then took his spot back in front of his untouched milkshake and cheeseburger.

I nodded to Stan and he said simply, "A book is missing from the Library of Atlantis."

Sherrie just turned white and her hand went to cover her mouth. Screamer shook his head and repeated what Stan and Madge had said.

"Now, time to fill in the new kid on the block," I said.

"First off, someone please tell me what the Library of Atlantis is?"

"It started as the great library of Atlantis," Stan said. "All the knowledge of the world from the time of Atlantis was stored in that great building."

"When Atlantis was destroyed," Patty said, "no one wanted to see all that knowledge go away, so with the help of hundreds of gods, the Gods of the Library protected the library with a vast dome sort of like this office, a half-turn out of phase with the real world."

"So where is this located now?" I asked, fearing that the answer would be under the Atlantic.

"Under about a hundred feet of rock in central Oregon," Stan said.

"Oregon?" I asked.

"It wasn't Oregon when they buried it," Stan said, not looking at me.

The Library of Atlantis was in Oregon. How strange was that? I would leave that bit of information until later to digest.

"So what is this library like now?" I asked.

"The problem came up about a century after Atlantis went down," Stan said. "The Gods of the Library decided since civilization was at a very low ebb, they would try to get at least one copy of every printed work in existence in the library. All written human knowledge in one place. So they started expanding and after another thousand years or so, they managed the task."

"Damn dumb idea," Screamer said, shaking his head.

"So what happened when they got all written human knowledge in one place?" I asked.

"No one really knows," Stan said. "Those a lot smarter than me say that it somehow tied together things about humanity that had never been tied together before, and created a powerful force that has been growing every century as millions more books are added into the library."

A couple things that I flat didn't understand, so I decided to ask the dumbest question first. "How does this library keep up with all the millions of books being published around the world today? And the electronic ones as well?"

"They just appear in the library," Ben said, a moment after he appeared in front of us. "They are already sorted and filed and the library expands as room is needed and the library shelves all of its own books now. No one ever really touches most of the books."

"Where is Laverne?" Stan asked as Ben sat down.

"Talking with the other gods who have been with the library from the beginning," Ben said, sitting down next to me in the booth. "They are all watching to see what will unravel first, try to stop it to buy more time."

"What is this unraveling?" I asked.

"From what I understand, you can think of it like a freeway," Stan said. "As long as all the traffic is moving along at the same speed, and the freeway can hold the number of cars at any moment, then nothing happens. But imagine one car suddenly stopping in one lane."

"A mess," I said. "So having one book missing will cause this?"

"And more," Screamer said. "It has never happened, but from what I'm told, a hell of a lot more."

Sherrie and Patty both nodded.

"And that's what is going to happen," Ben said, nodding. "It won't be pleasant for the human race and could set everything back by thousands of years."

"I hated the Dark Ages," Stan said.

I looked at him and made a note to ask him what exactly his job was in the Dark Ages. I don't think poker was in existence just yet.

"So this library is sort of magic," I said.

"Not magic anymore than nature and weather or your powers are magic," Ben said. "Just a force. A human binding force that has helped us for centuries."

"So did you ever think of asking the library what happened to the book?" I asked.

Silence.

So I decided to follow up with two more dumb questions. "And what book exactly is missing? And if no one touches anything anymore, how do you even know it's missing?"

Ben opened his mouth to answer, then shut it, clearly not having an answer to any of the three questions.

"Excuse me for a moment," he said, finally. He scooted out of the booth and vanished.

Seemed my three stupid questions might have hit a sore spot or two.

I glanced around at the four remaining. "Any of you ever seen this library?"

All of them shook their heads no.

I turned to Stan. "I don't have a library card, but I would love to see this place. Can you jump us there?"

He shook his head. "It's protected. Locked up tight."

Now that really bothered me. What was the point of having all written human knowledge in one place if humans couldn't even get to it?

That was one question I didn't think was so stupid.

CHAPTER THREE

"Mind calling Laverne?" I asked Stan. "I assume she could get us in the place."

"Why would you want to see such a vast repository of books?" Laverne asked, appearing in front of the table and again sitting down in a chair facing the table.

"Why do you keep all that knowledge locked away from the people who created it?" I asked. "Seems like the place shouldn't be called a library, but more like a book graveyard. It is underground, after all."

She frowned and said, "I don't know the answer to that question, but I will find out."

"Ask the library itself if it likes being locked away from people," I said, just as Laverne vanished.

Stan just shook his head. "As normal, your questions tend to get right to the heart of the problems."

"Only if no one knows the answers," I said, staring at my slowly getting cold cheeseburger and fries. My stomach was rumbling, but everyone considered this library thing a major disaster, so I figured that eating a normal lunch might be a little on the rude side.

I decided taking a sip of the melting milkshake might not be too far wrong, and maybe munching on a fry. I was just, deep down, having trouble taking one book being missing as a serious problem, especially since no one really knew what book it was that was missing.

A how-to-build-hydrogen-bombs book I might be concerned about, but a book on basket weaving, or a Zane Grey western would be another matter, even with this unraveling everyone seemed so afraid of, but had never seen in centuries.

I was about to take a second fry when I found myself standing near the center of a giant room, the polished marble ceiling towering far, far over my head.

I kind of choked down the first fry and gawked at the place.

The walls were at least three stories tall before curving up into the dome and were covered in dark wood bookcases, with walkways all the way around at every level, and the arches and pillars holding up the vast room were made of marble, polished to a shine.

The room had to be the size of a major college football stadium, and a hundred tunnels, at least, led off in all directions from this main room.

Stunning didn't even begin to describe this library.

The entire team was there, plus Laverne and Ben and a man in a long white robe with a long white beard I didn't recognize, but looked like he could have played the part of Gandalf in a Lord of the Rings movie.

We were the only ones in the big room, which could have easily had held a thousand people and looked like it was originally designed for this big floor to have couches and chairs and places for humans to sit and read. But now the floor was just a vast expanse of marble, with patterns drawn in the center.

"I am Thoth," the robed man said directly to me. "The head librarian."

I bowed slightly as I always do in front of gods I do not know. They seem to like the respect it shows them.

I noticed that all my team, including Stan, also bowed slightly. This guy must really be one of the old ones.

"An honor," I said.

"You have made an assumption that we can talk with the entity that is The Library of Atlantis," Thoth said. "We have never done so, or even thought of doing so. Why do you make such an assumption?"

I didn't want to tell him I was known for solving problems by asking really stupid questions until one stuck. So instead I said, "It seemed logical. If you don't mind, I would like to give it a try."

Thoth looked puzzled and looked at Laverne, who nodded.

"Please," Thoth said.

I moved away about ten paces to the center of the large room. A pattern on the floor there told me that it was an important spot.

I looked around, then said simply, "Library of Atlantis, may I ask you a question?"

"You may, Poker Boy," a voice said in normal tones. For some reason I had expected some booming movie-god voice that would echo, but I guess this was a library after all and booming voices would be too disruptive, if they ever let anyone in here to disrupt.

I glanced back at Thoth and Laverne and the team. All of them were staring wide-eyed at me.

"May I ask how a book became missing from your wonderful vastness?"

"No book is missing," the library said. "I simply hid one book, *2001: A Space Odyssey* by Clarke, from the librarians to see what reaction I might get."

I laughed. "Seems you got a good one."

"I did, didn't I," the Library of Atlantis said.

I swore I heard it chuckling.

"Why did you pick that book?" I asked. I had seen the movie, but never read the book.

"I liked the voice of Hal in the movie. Would you like me to speak like Hal?"

I laughed. "Please, no. Too scary."

Again I thought I heard the Library of Atlantis chuckling.

"Why haven't you talked with the librarians before now?" I asked.

"No one thought to talk with me."

I glanced back at where Thoth stood. He had lived in this place for centuries and never once asked the library a question. Might be time for him to retire.

"You are the accumulation of all the knowledge in all these books," I said to the library. "Correct?"

"I am."

"And you are hungry for more knowledge which is why you take in all books being produced today," I said. "Am I correct?"

"You are."

"Do you wish the librarians would let others in here to use your collection and talk with you?"

"I do," the library said.

"Would I be welcome back to study the history of the gods through all time?" I asked. "I need all the help I can get on that topic."

This time the library actually chuckled. "Poker Boy, you and your team are always welcome here, considering how many times all of you have saved the world."

"Thank you," I said. "And thanks for not disrupting the fabric of everything. Or whatever happens when a book goes missing."

The Library of Atlantis just kept chuckling. Finally it said, "That's a myth. It was started back when I first became aware and no one ever asked me if it was true."

Now it was my turn to laugh.

Finally I decided to ask one last question of the Library of Atlantis. "One more question," I said. "It might be stupid."

"Poker Boy, I doubt if any question you could ask would be stupid. It might show lack of a certain tidbit of knowledge, but never stupid. And knowledge is why I am here."

"Thank you," I said. "I am going to remember that. My question is simply this: Is there a god of the Internet and who is he or she?"

"There is no god yet of the Internet," The Library of Atlantis said. "But if you want my humble opinion, someone really should take that job since the Internet is here to stay in one form or another for a time."

I glanced back at my team and just smiled.

Stan shook his head and Patty actually laughed.

"Thank you, Library," I said. "I hope to return soon to your wonderful halls and see them full of questing minds."

"I have that same hope," the Library of Atlantis said. "And Poker Boy, thank you for asking the right question. With gaining knowledge, that is often far more important than the answer."

"That's good," I said, laughing "because it seems I am never short of questions."

With that, the Library of Atlantis chuckled so loud, it actually did echo.

A Reason To Play A Hunch

CHAPTER ONE

The Golden Nugget Casino poker room in Vegas felt a little tight for space, but the players were friendly and staff and dealers tended to smile more than normal around Las Vegas. That made up for a lot.

The entire room was decorated in soft brown and wood tones, with polished brass everywhere. It had over twenty tables with black padded rails and nine padded brown-leather chairs per table. Almost all of the chairs were full at the moment and there was a waiting list to get into some of the games.

In the back corner of the room, the remains of the afternoon tournament were still going. At time cheers or moans would fill the room from there. A good ten people stood around that table watching intently at every hand.

And even with all the people in the pretty small space, the

air was moving well and it wasn't even warm. That showed that the casino valued this poker room more than most casinos valued their poker rooms. They kept it updated, clean, staffed, and friendly. The perfect recipe for a successful room.

I normally didn't spend much time here at the Golden Nugget, but after working with my friends in the Ghost of a Chance agency on a problem we just wrapped up, I figured I would give the poker room a try.

The Ghost of a Chance agents tended to meet in the Golden Nugget Buffet up one floor from here and I had come to realize it was one of the top buffets in all of Las Vegas.

I also hadn't realized how much all the remodeling had done for the hotel and casino. It was as good as, if not better than, most hotels and casinos out on the Strip.

So in the last few days my girlfriend Patty, aka Front Desk Girl, and I had tried the buffet twice. And each time we had come down the escalator and gone to look at the poker room, Patty humoring me as we did.

After all, I was Poker Boy. Poker was what I did.

So now I was giving the poker room a try.

And so far I sure hadn't been disappointed. I was in a good five-ten no-limit game with only one local pro who didn't know me and six tourists bent on having a good time. Just about as perfect as it got.

It was interesting that when I had first become a superhero, when I was in Las Vegas, I always spent all my time at Binion's Casino across Fremont Street. I had met Patty there when she worked at the front desk of Binion's Hotel.

And Madge's diner, where the team used to meet in before we built my floating office, was only a block or so from here.

But I had never walked the fifty steps across Fremont Street to play here.

Now I wondered why I hadn't. Not only did this room feel like old times, but playing downtown felt like I had come home again. I liked that feeling.

I still had three hours left until Patty got off work at the MGM Grand and I was a good thousand up, just taking my time and enjoying the play.

The other pro at the table was about fifty years old, had a balding head, a wide grin, and a fun personality that hid his poker ability. After the first thirty minutes, we both just avoided each other where we could. There was more than enough to go around with the group at this table. Three men from Boise, two middle-aged women from somewhere in the Midwest, and one elderly man from Florida. All had money and wanted to enjoy spending it.

I was going to see if I could help with that enjoyment over the next few hours.

But suddenly it seemed that wasn't to be.

I was sitting with my back to a wall in the third spot on the table on the right side of the room. From that position I could see most of the room, the main entrance, as well as everyone I was playing against.

A guy, wearing a suit that looked like it was right out of the 1940s stood off to one side of the large archway entrance to the poker room, sort of watching everything. I hadn't seen him come up to the entrance.

He was handsome in a Rock Hudson sort of way, thin and almost dapper, with that classic movie-star chin.

And the more I looked at him the more my warning bells were going off big time. Not danger bells, just warning bells. But he didn't look to be trouble.

I studied him a little closer. He stood maybe five-nine and had a real Fedora on his head that looked to be felt and expensive and he knew how to wear it.

It looked like his natural style, not some costume.

He just flat looked out of place.

Then my little voice changed that to "Out of time."

I knew right then my night of friendly poker was more than likely over.

Chapter Two

I tossed away the two cards in my hand and stood, working my way through the crowd of chairs and tables to the front, not really looking directly at the guy, but not letting him out of my sight either.

As I cleared the last table near the wide archway entrance, the sounds of the casino beyond got louder, like I was walking upstream against a torrent of noise.

The guy hadn't moved, but as I stepped closer to walk past him, he glanced at me and nodded.

I nodded back.

"You got time to talk for a second, Poker Boy?" the man asked, his voice level and low.

Now my heart was really racing. The only people who knew who I really was were on my team or other superheroes and gods. And a few of the Ghost of a Chance agents.

"Sure," I said, stopping to face him and he turned to face me. "Don't think we've met?"

"We haven't," the man said. "But we need to talk in private if you don't mind. No one can see me but you. I don't want people thinking you are talking with yourself."

I laughed. "Appreciate that."

I stopped time around the two of us, making everyone freeze suddenly. I actually didn't stop time. From my understanding, no one can do that, not even the most powerful gods. I just took us between moments in time, which had the effect of looking like I had stopped time.

The most striking thing to me every time I used this power was how all sound suddenly stopped. The noisy casino went instantly silent. Everyone frozen.

And trust me, no one looked good in a frozen face.

The guy nodded but didn't seem surprised at stepping between instants of time. "Thanks. I thought you might be able to both see me and help me."

"See you?" I asked.

He reached around and put his hand through the wall and then pulled it back out. "I'm what is called a ghost I suppose."

"You an agent?" I asked.

"Of what?" he asked, looking clearly confused for the first time.

I decided quickly to ignore that and just back up the conversation since it seemed this guy was a real ghost, something I didn't realize could exist outside of the Ghost of a Chance agents.

"Do you have a name and do you know when you died?" I asked, trying my best to keep my heart from pounding right out of my chest. Over the last years I had run into some weird situations, but this was one of the weirdest so far. And that was going some.

Weird and strange tended to go hand-in-hand with the superheroes and gods.

"Lawrence Oakes," he said. "But all my friends used to call me Larry."

He pointed up toward the old hotel tower. "I died upstairs in a room on the sixth floor in 1951. Ticker gave out. Me and my wife Bettie had just celebrated in the old-fashioned way our fifth wedding anniversary, if you get my drift. I had just dressed to go out for dinner."

He shook his head, clearly thinking about the moment. I wasn't real sure I wanted to hear much more but before I could ask another question he went on.

"Bettie was looking really sweet when she came out of the bathroom. She was a stunning woman. My entire life. Then she found me slumped over the bed and started screaming. I just stood off to one side when I realized what had happened and that I couldn't help her or comfort her."

For a moment I thought Larry was going to tear up, then he took a deep breath.

"I just stood and watched the woman I love cry and then they came and took her away and my body away and I stayed.

I always wondered how she did after that, what her life was like."

"And what have you been doing ever since?" I asked, almost afraid of the answer.

"Just hanging around and watching the people and the hotel change," he said. "Not sure why I didn't catch a ride out of here on the light. I've watched others die here and they all get a ride. When I saw you and that beautiful girlfriend of yours in the buffet, I knew you two were special and might be able to help me get a ride to the other side if you could see me. I just played a hunch about it when she called you Poker Boy."

So that's how he knew my name. But I was a lowly super-hero. No chance I could help him. But I might be able to find some people who could.

"You mind if I call in some help?" I asked.

"Just glad to be able to talk with someone again," he said, shrugging. "More help the better in my book."

"Stan, Ben, could you join me for a moment?"

This was going to be fun getting their take on this very strange situation. Maybe they would have some answers.

At this point, I sure had none.

CHAPTER THREE

S tan, the God of Poker and my immediate boss appeared an instant after I called him. He had on his normal dull clothes. A sweater-vest, tan slacks, and a light shirt under the vest. He looked to be of that indeterminate age even though I knew he had been alive during the time of Atlantis. The guy was so good at looking bland that he could vanish in a crowd and no one would give him a second look.

A moment later Ben, one of the gods of libraries and of knowledge appeared. Ben looked like he belonged in a library. He had the old professor look with the rumpled white hair and the small glasses. He was by far the smartest man I had ever met about everything, including the history of the gods and superheroes.

"Stan, Ben, this is Larry Oakes," I said, introducing my

two team members to the ghost. "He died here in 1951 and has just been hanging around ever since."

"Oh, no," Ben said, shaking his head. "Something has gone totally wrong."

Stan just nodded, showing no emotion since as the God of Poker he was the master of no emotion.

Larry shrugged, clearly knowing after over sixty-five years roaming the Golden Nugget Casino that something had gone wrong.

I decided to ask Larry a few more questions to give Stan and Ben time to process what had just been tossed at them.

"Larry, have you ever been out of this building?"

"Didn't know I could," Larry said, shrugging as if that actually didn't matter. "Mostly I only move around at night when there are fewer people because having someone walk through me is very strange. I can read their thoughts and I don't really want to know what most of these people are thinking."

I nodded at that. I didn't blame him in the slightest. The Ghost Agents I had worked with said that being inside people's minds took them a long time to get used to.

"Larry," Ben said, "it sounds like you were intended to be a Ghost of a Chance agent and no one came to train you."

Larry just shook his head. "Second time I have heard that Ghost Agent thing. What are they?"

I quickly explained to Larry that certain people with certain skills who died were picked to be part of a team of Ghost Agents. Their job was to help people.

"So you telling me," Larry said, "that I've been hanging around for sixty-five years doing nothing because someone screwed up?"

Ben nodded. "It appears that way."

Larry just shook his head.

The silence of the frozen casino around us seemed to get very heavy. I was about to break the silence with another stupid question when Larry sighed and said, "Don't suppose we can do anything about what has happened. So how about getting me a ride out of here and to the other side? Wouldn't mind seeing Bettie again."

"Don't think you are going to want to do that?" a voice said from beside me.

I glanced over at Laverne, Lady Luck herself. She was one of the most powerful gods and seemed to run every-thing. She was the one who had put my team of gods and superheroes with the Ghost Agents at times to save the world.

She was also the one who had given me the power to even see ghosts in the first place.

"Larry," I said, acting calm as if the most powerful god in all the world appeared beside me all the time, "this is Laverne."

Larry nodded. "Nice meeting you. But why would you say I might not want to leave yet?"

"Because," Lady Luck said, smiling, "you haven't been waiting to leave, you have been waiting for your partner to join you."

"I only have one partner," Larry said, shaking his head, almost angry. "And I'm sure Bettie is long dead by now."

"She's not," Lady Luck said. "At least not until one week from tomorrow when she will join you."

At that moment two of the top Ghost Agents appeared beside Lady Luck.

"I'm sure these two will explain everything to you," Laverne said, nodding. "I hope to see you again."

She vanished.

Then Ben and Stan also vanished without a word leaving me standing there between instants of time with three ghosts. Again, weird didn't begin to describe my job at times.

Jewel and Tommy both introduced themselves to Larry.

Both Jewel and Tommy were dressed in their normal evening clothes of jeans, dress shirts, and sneakers. They were a handsome couple, both in their mid-twenties when they died. She had been a doctor, he had been a cop. In the five years since they died they had become the top Ghost Agents.

"I've seen you two in the buffet a lot," Larry said.

Jewel nodded. "We are also ghosts. We knew you were here, but our bosses didn't think we should talk to you just yet."

"Why is that?" Larry asked a half second before I could.

I was starting to get the idea that Larry being on his own here had been part of a plan, not a screw-up.

"Because," Jewel said, "they want to recruit both you and Bettie to our team and Bettie won't pass over for another week."

"Why would Bettie want to spend time with me after all these years?" Larry asked.

"Because she's never gotten over you," Tommy said. "She raised your son and your grandchildren and never met another man. She didn't want another man. She waited for you just as you have been waiting here for her."

Larry looked shocked for the first time since I had seen him. "I had a son?"

Tommy nodded. "Born about nine months after you died."

"And three grandchildren and four great-grandchildren so far," Jewel said, smiling.

I could feel I was smiling as well. Damn hard to keep a poker face in this kind of situation.

I thought for a moment Larry was going to just slump to the floor, but then somehow he pulled himself together. This guy was a lot stronger than I would have been in the same situation.

"Can I see them?" Larry asked.

"After Bettie joins you," Jewel said. "She will look the same as the day you died, just as you still look the same. That is the time she imprinted on just as you did."

"So how come," I said, "someone couldn't tell Larry here all this back in 1951?"

Jewel smiled at me. "I asked the same question. It was because they both had to prove they were meant to be a ghost team together forever."

"Unlike how Jewel and I died in the same car wreck,"

Tommy said, "Many teams die years apart. You met Gail and the Sunset Kid?"

I nodded. Nice couple. Clearly in love and working up in Portland.

"They died almost a hundred years apart," Tommy said. "The Sunset Kid had to basically just work alone for all those years until Gail arrived."

"So if Bettie had met another man and moved on?" Larry asked.

"Then a Ghost Agent would have contacted you and trained you at that point," Jewel said. "But just as you waited, Bettie also waited."

"So guess my job here didn't much matter," I said, laughing.

"Actually," Jewel said, "you just gave us an extra week to get Larry ready is all. The plan was to contact him next week."

"Well," I said, laughing, "glad to be of some help."

I looked directly at Larry. "After you and Bettie are both trained and settled down together, I really want to meet this special woman. And I am sure Patty would as well."

"Oh, trust me, it will be our pleasure," Larry said. "Thank you."

"To the buffet for dinner?" Tommy asked.

Jewel nodded.

At that all three ghosts vanished, leaving me standing there alone with a bunch of frozen people all around me.

Yeah, nothing strange at all about my job.

I tried to remember exactly where I was and in what position I had been when I froze time and then dropped back into the real flow, letting the sounds of the casino smash in around me.

I turned and headed back toward the table where my chips sat. It looked like I might actually get to enjoy the night after all.

As I sat down, one of the guys from Boise asked me why I was smiling so big.

"Sometimes things just go right," I said, laughing.

"Yeah," the guy said, "playing poker in this place is just about as right at is gets."

And to that I could only nod and smile some more.

MYSTERY CAT

Chapter 1

I love lunches in my invisible floating office over the Strip in Las Vegas. You just never knew who was going to show up at noon every day just to enjoy one of Madge's amazing hamburgers and sit and talk.

And in Vegas, it seemed the sun was always shining, so the four glass walls of floor-to-ceiling windows of my office often made it seem like we were actually outside, just sitting in a brightly-lit diner booth floating on a small platform.

I loved my office. Not sure if I ever said that. And it seemed from the different members of the team who stopped by regularly for lunch, everyone did as well, including Lady Luck herself, Laverne, who showed up a couple times a week at least.

On a normal day, as if there ever was such a thing in the superhero universe, the group for lunch included Stan, the

God of Poker and my direct boss. Stan never seemed to wear anything but a tan sweater and tan pants and was maybe the blandest and calmest man alive.

Ben, the oldest and smartest of the superheroes, usually showed up as well. He was the only god I had ever met who looked like an old guy, actually an old librarian. The rest of us had just basically stopped aging at thirty. No idea how old Ben actually was, but he was part of the major group that went all the way back more thousands of years than I want to think about.

Patty and I also never seemed to miss a lunch. Patty Ledgerwood, aka Front Desk Girl, was my partner in all things superhero and love and sharing. She was also my best friend and the person who kept me calm and anchored, especially in times when the team had to save the world. We had been a couple for years now and I still had no idea why such a beautiful and powerful woman stayed with me.

Today she was in her MGM Grand uniform and was on her lunch break, her long brown hair pulled back and off her face. It was about ten minutes before noon and she and I were just standing near one wall of my office, talking and watching the cars and tourists below on the Strip. Madge hadn't appeared yet from her diner down off Fremont to see who was around.

There was a doorway from my floating office to a side passage in Madge's diner that allowed those who couldn't teleport to get to my office. And Madge used the door to bring us all food every day.

Suddenly, as we stood there, my warning sense went off that something was wrong. That sense (along with teleporting, slipping between moments of time, and asking stupid questions) was one of my main superpowers.

I glanced around. Nothing in the office, so had to be below.

"Spidey sense just went off," I said to Patty as I turned to study the city below us.

Patty did the same.

For what seemed like an eternity, but had to have been only thirty or so seconds, we studied all the people, cars, and buildings below us. I couldn't see a thing wrong, which is saying something for the Las Vegas Strip. Not even the standard staggering overweight man wearing a bright Hawaiian shirt, shorts, tall white socks, black dress shoes, and carrying a four-foot-high drink.

Nothing.

Finally Patty pointed and said, "There!"

I saw nothing.

"Beside the second palm from the intersection in the middle of the street on the median."

I found the second palm, but still couldn't see what she thought was wrong until a colored orange, brown, and black area near the base of the palm moved and started to dash into the street, right in front of a lot of traffic.

It was a cat with only seconds to live.

"No!" Patty shouted.

I instantly put both of us out of time, stopping the mad

dash of the cat and the traffic that was about to end the cat's life.

Then I jumped to the cat in the street. Being in front of frozen cars barreling down on me was not fun. If my stepping between moments of time power slipped, I would end up as a hood ornament.

It was creepy being in the middle of that kind of traffic and there was no sound. None.

And since I hadn't been outside for days, I hadn't realized just how hot it was, especially on that pavement. No wonder the cat was making a run for it.

I grabbed the cat out of mid-stride, tucked it under my arm, and jumped back to the coolness of my office.

"Thank you," Patty said.

Patty wanted to take the cat from me but I shook my head. No way she wanted to be holding a terrified cat when I released us all back into time. And I didn't either, so I sat the cat on the ground, aimed away from the closest glass wall, and released Patty and I back into normal time.

The cat made it almost instantly about halfway across my office before it realized something had changed and stopped, frozen and scared to death.

Then it ran under the booth to hide in the dark right were we were planning to have lunch.

Patty laughed and hugged me. "My hero," she said.

"So now we not only save the world, we save cats and dogs."

"We're going to need some help with this one," Patty said,

looking under the booth and talking softly. Then she looked back at me. "Might want to get that superhero of cats you helped a few months back."

"I'll see if she wants to join us for lunch. Be right back."

And with that I jumped to see if I could find Pakhet Jones.

CHAPTER 2

It took me two stops before I found Pakhet Jones. My first stop was to knock on the door at Marble Grant and Sims in the Ogden Condominiums in the downtown area. The only time I had met Pak was there when I helped her rescue a cat from an impossible situation.

Marble, a ghost agent that I could see, appeared in the hallway beside me, looking as stunning as ever in a silk blouse, jeans, and running shoes. She and her partner and love, Sims, would spend their days looking for people to help by crawling inside people's minds.

If I had to wake up every day thinking I would do nothing but be inside other people's minds, I would never get out of bed. But it seems that Marble and Sims and other ghost agents flat loved it. And they helped a lot of people with that power, that was for sure.

Marble told me that Pak had a condo two floors up from hers. And if she wasn't there, try Cabana #7 at the Mandalay Casino pool. It seemed that Pak basically owned that cabana and used it like an office most every day. And that Marble and Sims really enjoyed joining her there at times.

I jumped to outside of Pak's condo and knocked and a moment later the most amazingly beautiful woman answered the door. She saw me and beamed.

"Poker Boy. What a wonderful surprise. Come on in."

With that she turned and led the way back into her white and gold condo with a fantastic view of the entire city of Las Vegas.

Pak was a striking woman in any circumstance, standing over six feet tall and very thin. Her skin was a rich golden color and she was completely bald, with her face and head also a beautiful golden shade.

She had on a black bikini that left little to any imagination and was covered only by a sheer white cover-up that hung open and made the entire look breathtaking.

I know it took my breath away, because it was a ways into her condo before I could say anything.

The black-and-white cat that I had helped her rescue was stretched out in the sun in her living room area and didn't even bother to look up at me.

"I could use your help with a cat," I said.

I told her what had happened and where the cat was a few minutes ago when I left.

"On the Strip?" Pak asked. "There are no homes anywhere near there."

"Some condos a ways south is all," I said.

"So a cat with a mystery," she said, nodding. "Let me slip some clothes over this. I was just about to head to my cabana office."

She vanished through a door as I turned to stare out over the city. Again the cat that I had helped rescue from nearly dying didn't even bother to open an eye and look at me. It even ignored my growling stomach that right now wanted nothing more than a good hamburger and fries and vanilla shake for lunch.

Less than a minute later, Pak came back out wearing a light tan blouse and jeans and running shoes, nearly the same outfit that Marble Grant had been wearing.

"I'll jump us," I said.

And a moment later we were in my office floating over the Strip.

Patty was sitting on the floor in front of the booth clearly trying to comfort the cat. Stan and Ben both stood off to one side looking amused at the entire situation.

I introduced Pak to Patty, then turned to introduce Stan and Ben.

But Pak said, "Ben! Stan! Wonderful to see you both."

Then she hugged them.

I just shook my head. Amazing sometimes how small the god and superhero world was. I would have to ask them later how they knew each other.

Then Pak seemed to realize where she was at and just sort of stopped and looked around, her mouth open.

I smiled. My office tended to do that to people.

Finally she shook her head and looked at the booth. "Is that out of Madge's place down off of Fremont?"

"A replica," I said.

"Might as well be in my place," Madge said, appearing from the invisible door on the other side of the booth. "Good seeing you young woman. You want your normal when this is all finished?"

"I would love that," Pak said, smiling. "Thanks."

Then Pak got down on her hands and knees where Patty had been sitting and looked in under the table.

"So who do we have here?" she said aloud to the cat hunched fearfully as far back in the booth as it could get.

Pak nodded. Then glanced back at me. "His name is Table Stakes, but his human companion just called him Stakes."

That shocked me. That was a poker term, which meant his owner, or companion as cats like to think of the humans they live with, must be a poker player.

"I understand you had an adventure outside," Pak said to the cat. "What were you doing there?"

I knew that Pak could hear the thoughts of cats, but that left the rest of us to try to figure out a one-sided conversation, like she was talking on the phone and we couldn't hear the person on the other end.

Pak nodded after a moment and sat back, turning to look

up at the rest of us standing around the room. The look on her face was of anger and worry.

"Stake's companion was drugged and taken by two men from their home. Stake tried to scratch and attack one of the men and was tossed in the trunk of a car with his companion. Stake got out by crawling through the back seat and out a slightly open back window. That was just before you rescued him."

All I could do was stand there and stare.

"Stake believes his companion might be hurt."

At that moment the cat named Stakes, a beautiful and small calico, came out from under the booth and crawled into Pak's lap.

Pak nodded. "We'll do what we can."

Clearly talking to the cat.

Chapter 3

I had no idea what to do next. Not one clue. We had a cat who had no idea where he lived, no idea of what color or make a car was, and no way to identify two men who might have hurt a poker player for who knew what reason.

The silence in my office didn't feel normal, that was for sure. Everyone was trying to puzzle this one out.

Finally Pak said to the cat, "How far from where Poker Boy rescued you were you when you escaped the car?"

Pak nodded, then looked up. "Stakes escaped right at the spot you rescued him, but the car he escaped from was going the other way than the ones threatening him."

I nodded. "So the car was going southbound, which means more than likely he came out a back window on the driver's side."

Pak stood and handed Stakes to Patty, who cuddled him and nodded, clearly using her calming powers on the cat to keep it relaxed.

"I got a detective friend," Pak said, "who can get access to cameras that might have seen it. He owes me."

"Superhero?" I asked.

"No," she said, pulling out her phone and hitting a listing. "Just a really nice guy, good cop, nearing retirement."

After a moment she said, "Detective Halligan. It is Pakhet Jones."

She nodded and again we were listening to a one-sided conversation she was having.

"I have a cat problem and I need your help. Are there traffic cams along the Strip?"

She nodded. "Every foot of it? Good, I was hoping for that."

I quickly gave her the address that was right near where the cat escaped.

"A car, going southbound on the Strip, had a cat escape out the back driver's window." She gave him the address, then added, "We really need to find the owner of that car."

"Don't ask," she said after a moment. "Can you just get me the owner of that car's name and address? I'll owe you."

After a moment she said, "Thanks."

She looked around. "Figured it was better at this point to not bring in the possible hurt person until we knew for sure."

I nodded. "Tough to explain."

"It won't take him long," she said, moving over to pet

Stakes as Patty held him. Clearly the cat was in heaven at the moment, his paws going in and out.

Less than one minute later her phone played the theme from Hawaii Five-O and she answered it.

"Any luck, Detective?"

She nodded. "Benson Little." And then she repeated the address as if she was writing it down so we all heard it. And then the make of the car. A blue, four-door Buick sedan. Three years old.

But I didn't need all of that. I knew Benson Little from one too many times playing at a poker table with him. The guy was an easy mark, had more tells than a billboard, and just wasn't fun to be around.

And he always had a faint odor of mold and rot on his clothes.

Stan was also shaking his head at the name. He clearly knew Benson as well.

Pak thanked the detective and hung up.

"How bad is this guy, really?" I asked Stan.

"Dangerous," was all that Stan said.

I turned to Patty. "Would you and Ben stay with Stakes?"

Patty nodded.

"Stan, you want to take us to his house out of time?"

Stan nodded and a moment later Stan and I and Pak were standing in the heat of the afternoon in front of the address the detective had given her. It was a single-story run-down home that had seen its last good days in the '80s and been ignored ever since. Pealing paint, nothing but weeds and rocks in the yard. And a closed garage door.

"Inside the garage," I said to Stan and he jumped us there.

Frozen in place were Benson Little and another minor-level poker player who lost more than he won and I had never bothered to remember his name.

They were in the process of lifting professional poker player Jonathan Richard out of the trunk of the car.

Jonathan was a great guy, liked by everyone, and deadly in live high-stakes games. His wife had died a few years ago, and I remember half of the Las Vegas poker community showed up for the funeral.

"Damn it!" Stan said.

"Let's find some wire and whatever to tie these two idiots up," I said.

Pak and I went to what looked like a long unused workbench and found enough zip ties and twine to make sure both men wouldn't move or get away.

The three of us took Jonathan and moved him to a spot on the garage floor, then tied up the other two and put nasty-smelling, oil-covered rags over their eyes and left them sitting on the ground against the dirty car.

"Okay," I said. "Drop us back into time."

Stan released us back into regular time and the sounds of the neighborhood smashed in.

Then Stan and Pak both worked to see if Jonathan was alive.

Thankfully, he was.

"I'll get an ambulance here," Pak said. "After I call Detective Halligan."

"What the hell is going on?" Benson shouted, struggling to get free, but doing nothing but tightening the twine around his wrists and legs. His partner just sat there shaking.

Stan, as calm as any god could be, stood and moved over to Benson, then without even a hesitation or even saying a word, tipped him over and kicked him squarely in the groin.

The sound Benson made was not a sound I ever wanted to hear again. But I laughed and so did Pak. Stan just nodded, calm and collected as you would expect from the God of Poker.

CHAPTER 4

Thankfully Jonathan awoke just before Detective Halligan got there, so he could explain what Benson and his partner had done and why. Seems they had heard he had a bunch of cash in a safe in his house and they wanted it. They forced him to open the safe and then knocked him out with some sort of drug.

The cash was in a bag with other personal stuff from Jonathan's home on the kitchen table. Jonathan was pretty sure they were going to kill him. Benson had laughed that Jonathan would be just fine in the backyard with the others. So it seemed the police had some digging to do back in the weeds.

Jonathan, right before the ambulance hauled him away, asked me how we had found him. Detective Halligan seemed real interested in that answer as well.

I pointed to Pak. "They tossed Stakes into the trunk with you and he got out and I rescued him and Pak there knew to call Detective Halligan and how to track what needed to be tracked. She is amazing with cats."

"Stakes all right?" Jonathan asked, looking suddenly worried.

"He's in great hands," I said, not lying in the slightest.

So by the time we got back to my office for lunch, it was well after two.

Patty and Ben were sitting in the booth, clearly finished eating, and Stakes was on Patty's lap munching on a fry.

Pak looked at Stake and said, "You companion is going to be all right. He should be home in a few days. You can stay with me until then."

She nodded and then turned as Madge came in to take our lunch orders.

"What did Stakes say?" I asked.

Pak just laughed as Stakes kept working on the fry.

"He said, 'Good.'"

"That was all he said?" I asked. "I saved his life and we saved his companion's life and all he says is 'Good.'"

"Cats are creatures of few words," Pak said, smiling as she slid into the booth beside Ben.

Patty touched my leg and smiled, "Don't take it personally, just because you aren't."

Ben and Stan both laughed.

I honestly had no idea how to take that.

PLAYING SCARED

CHAPTER ONE

I flat hated it when someone played with scared money.

Scared money is when a player can't afford to be betting what he has in front of him, but for some reason he or she feels they need to play.

You tended to see scared money players at times in Las Vegas. I hated it every time I did.

I was in what had been a really nice, easy-going five-ten no limit game in the poker room at the MGM Grand. I liked the room with the brown cloth and leather furnishings, the excess of plants, and high ceilings. The casino was just far enough away to keep the sound down and very little second-hand smoke got near the place.

Plus the room had its share of tourists, good players, and a few professionals like me. Kenyon, an older grinder of a pro sat directly across from me in the three chair and we had so far managed to stay out of each other's way, being happy to just enjoy the game and take the money from the tourists.

Another reason I liked playing in this room was that my girlfriend, Patty Ledgerwood, aka Front Desk Girl, worked about fifty paces away around the corner at the front desk of the hotel. When she got off work, she would just wonder into the room, let me finish a hand, and then we would head for our wonderful condo.

Patty and I had been together for some years now and I loved her now more than when I first met her. I couldn't imagine being a superhero with her at my side.

So far tonight I was about a grand up in two hours and feeling pretty good when this guy who looked about forty or so, with a blue Izod golf shirt and nice silk slacks, put a rack of chips on the table in front of the sixth chair, two over from my position. Five hundred, a decent buy-in to the game. He dressed like he could afford it.

He had short-cut brown hair, deep dark eyes, and he looked nervous. My warning voice went off almost instantly and I tried to get a better read on the guy as he stacked his chips and then couldn't figure out what to do with the little plastic rack.

The dealer, a nice woman by the name of Connie, caught the guy's problem and extended her hand and took the rack from him. He looked actually relieved.

This guy did not belong at this table. More than likely he had played some home-game poker, maybe read a book or two on no-limit poker, and figured he could do it in Las Vegas.

Normally, I would be excited to see someone like him show up. It would be like free money, but this guy bothered me.

I glanced down the table at Kenyon and he was staring at the guy and frowning as well. He looked up, caught my eye, and shrugged. The new guy bothered Kenyon as well, clearly.

I turned my attention to the guy and focused harder, trying to get any kind of read on him. No danger from him. Just fear and desperation was all I was getting.

So why was five hundred in chips causing a guy who looked healthy and wore silk slacks and an expensive golf shirt to be desperate? Made no sense.

For the next half hour, the new guy played very few hands. He mostly just sat and watched and sweated slightly, working at a bottle of water like it was his last meal.

When he did come into a plot, his hand shook a little and he under bet. Normally I would just call him to see what he had, and so would Kenyon, but we both dropped out as did everyone else and let him rake the small pot. He looked relieved, again not a good sign.

Ten minutes later Kenyon called it a night, shaking his head and leaving with his winnings.

Patty didn't get off work for another two hours, so I decided to just stick it out and see what happened. My little voice was telling me the guy needed some help, but not a clue what kind of help that might be.

Thirty minutes later the guy had lost two hands and he was down about a hundred and fifty and looking almost panicked. I hadn't played a hand against him. He was, at best, a mediocre player, the kind I normally loved to see approach a table with a large rack of chips.

And the game was no longer fun. I was about to cash out when I glanced up and saw Marble and Sims coming walking from the lobby area.

Now Marble Grant and her partner, Sally Glass, aka Sims, were both ghost agents. No one else could see them, but I could. They had both been superheroes and good friends of Patty when they died and luckily had been recruited to be ghost agents. And they were two of the best.

And they both were stunningly good-looking and very much in love. Both were tall and thin and they usually wore jeans and expensive blouses. Marble seemed to change her hair color with the day of the week, tonight being streaks of red, while Sims had long blonde hair that she let go down her back most times.

I waved at them to stop and excused myself from the table and went over near a white marble column that was part of the decorations of the MGM Grand. Then instead of pretending to talk on a phone since no one else could see them, I took the three of us out of time. Actually, I just slipped us between an instant of time, one of my most favorite superpowers.

All the sound around us vanished as everyone froze.

"Damn I want to learn how to do that someday," Marble said, glancing around.

"Would sure come in handy," Sims said, smiling.

"So I assume you might need our help on something," Marble said, glancing back at the table where I had been.

"What?" Sims asked, smiling at Marble. "A superhero can't just want to talk to a couple of ghost agents?"

"Oh, I suppose," Marble said, laughing. Then she turned to me, trying to be serious and failing. "How's the weather?"

I laughed and pointed to the table. "See the guy with short hair sitting two away from where I was?"

"Blue shirt?" Sims asked.

"He's got something going wrong and damned if I can figure out what it might be."

Marble nodded. "Allow me. Might be interesting. His aura tells me he's a good guy."

She moved across the room to the guy and vanished inside him.

Ghost agents have the ability to read people's thoughts and often control their actions without the person knowing it. But I had to admit, every time I saw a ghost agent go inside another person, it sort of made me feel weird. Something like that shouldn't be possible, but at times like this I was glad it was.

A moment later Marble appeared and her smile was gone. I don't think I had ever seen Marble Grant without a smile on her face.

"Oh, oh," Sims said softly as Marble moved back toward us through the frozen room of people and the silence.

That worried me more than I wanted to think about.

CHAPTER TWO

"So how bad?" Sims asked before I could say anything.

"Bad," Marble said. "The guy's wife has been kidnapped."

"And he's trying to win the ransom?" I asked, stunned at that kind of stupidity.

"It's worse," Marble said. "It seems the guy there, whose name is John Higgins, is a columnist and wrote a column about how poker is a sucker's game and not a sport at all."

I shook my head. "Typical opinion of someone who doesn't know anything about poker. So why is that important?"

"Guess young Higgins there made the wrong poker player angry as he kept up his assault on the game and even threatened to write a book about it," Marble said.

"So Higgins is an idiot," I said. "There are a lot of them. What is he doing here now?"

"To get his wife back," Marble said, "he has to take five hundred dollars to this very table with you sitting at it and actually play as best he knows how and not lose all the money in four hours."

I was shocked at that. I'm known as being a good player around the city, but clearly someone knew more about me than I felt comfortable with. And I was going to need to figure that out as soon as we got Higgins' wife safely back.

"So he's being watched," Sims said, looking around the room.

"I agree," I said. "I'll go back to the game and see if I can feed Higgins some money through a few hands. Can you two scan this crowd?"

Both of them nodded.

"Don't miss anyone," I said. "Other players, crew, everyone, to see if you can find the spotter? We need to know where to find his wife before we do anything."

"We got it," Marble said.

Sims nodded. "There might be more than one."

Marble and I both agreed to that.

I released myself and Marble and Sims back into the flow of time and all the accompanying noise, then I moved back to the table.

Marble and Sims were making fast work of checking out the others inside the poker room, going in and out of people like dolphins jumping in the water.

Higgins came into the very next hand with a slight raise and I just called him. He looked panicked at that.

Everyone else dropped out, so he and I were heads-up.

He bet out again after the flop, too small, a rookie mistake. I again just called him.

He checked the next card and I checked and he also checked the last card and I did as well. He showed two pair, a solid hand that would have won no matter what.

"Nice hand," I said, flipping my cards into the muck without showing him that I had nothing.

He looked relieved as he pulled the chips toward his small stack.

At that moment a middle-aged guy with about a thousand in chips sat down in Kenyon's old seat and professionally stacked his chips, putting the rack on the rail beside him to be picked up.

The guy wore a wrinkled suit jacket with no tie, and his hair looked slightly greasy.

I instantly got a bad feeling about the guy. And Higgins glanced at him and then just stared down at his chips.

At that moment Marble came out of a guy two tables over and pointed. "Got one," she shouted over the noise.

Only Sims and I could hear her, luckily.

I nodded at the guy who had just sat down and Marble caught my meaning and came over to him and vanished into the guy.

A moment later Marble appeared, standing beside the guy. "He's the mastermind of the entire thing. There are only the two of them here and I know where Higgin's wife is. We'll go get her safe, help her identify the two, and bring the police back."

I nodded and a few second later she and Sims jumped away.

Now it was up to me to keep these guys busy for a short time.

On the next hand, the greasy-haired guy came in with a strong raise. I didn't even look at my cards, but just called him.

"Playing in the dark," the guy said, sneering as everyone else on the table folded.

"Against you I don't need to play any other way," I said, smiling.

Then I glanced at Higgins. "Always people who think they know at lot about poker, but really know nothing."

Higgins' face turned white and the guy at the end of the table snorted and got slightly angry.

I turned and stared at the guy as he watched the flop hit the table. I knew instantly he had missed.

But he made a strong bet and I pushed in all my chips.

"All in."

He sat back hard. For him to call me, he would have to wager the entire thousand he had just brought to the table.

"How can you do that without even looking at your cards?" he demanded.

"I don't need to," I said calmly. "You missed the flop and

just about anything I might have will beat the garbage you are bluffing with."

He stared at me, then huffed and tossed his cards into the muck.

As I raked the pot, I glanced at Higgins. Then I said softly so the guy at the other end couldn't hear, "This is a game of money and power. Before you write more about something you don't know about, you might want to learn. Knowledge will keep you out of trouble in the future, both in life and on the poker table."

His face went completely white and he said nothing. Clearly he thought I was with the kidnappers.

It took three more hands before the police arrived. They came in with hands on their guns and arrested both men, handcuffed them, and had read them their rights before they got them out of the poker room.

A moment later Higgins' wife appeared with another officer and Higgins jumped up and ran to her.

Marble and Sims appeared beside me.

"They had her in a van in the parking lot here, tied up and gagged," Marble said as everyone in the room watched the scene of the reunion.

"They had no intention of hurting her," Sims said. "Just wanted to teach her husband a lesson."

"She identified them," Marble said.

"There are easier ways to teach lessons," I said. "Most poker rooms give lessons for free."

Marble and Sims both laughed.

The woman officer finally led Higgins wife away and Higgins started to leave with another officer to follow her without getting his money off the table.

"Might want to come back and get this," I said to him. "You know where she will be."

The officer waiting for him nodded that it was all right.

Higgins glanced back at me and again his face went white as he came toward the table.

I laughed. "I wasn't with them. I was the one who spotted that something was wrong."

"How?" Higgins asked as one of the staff racked up his chips for him. I doubted the poor guy could have done it.

"Honestly," I said, "You have the world's worst poker face. You didn't belong in this game, and looked like you were playing with scared money, so I knew something was wrong. Some friends did some investigating and we figured it out."

He nodded, shaking his head. "To this day I have no idea why I wrote those articles about poker."

I shrugged. "Most poker players know what the game really is. Unlike those two idiots, we don't have to prove it to anyone."

"Thank you," he said. "And thank your friends for me as well."

Marble and Sims just smiled and bowed slightly.

"Oh, you just did," I said, laughing. "Now stay out of a poker room until you are ready."

He just shook his head. "I doubt my wife will ever let me mention poker again."

"Can't say as I blame her," Marble said.

With that Higgins took his money and followed the police officer out.

"Well, that was fun," Marble said.

"It sure was," Sims said. "Any time you need us, Poker Boy, you just call."

"I sure will," I said, trying not to let anyone see me standing and talking to myself.

They jumped away and I turned back to the table. It was still over an hour until Patty got off work.

I still had a few good hands left in the evening. And a few more dollars to win.

A Beautiful History

Chapter One

I was sitting peacefully on a very comfortable chair of thick cushions and soft cloth near the MGM Poker Room. The chair sat off in a slight nook near a large column and from there I could not only watch some of the games going on in the poker room, but see the tourists passing by.

Everyone seemed so happy, enjoying their vacations. I liked to just soak in that feeling at times. It sort of recharged me, even though I got most of my powers from just being in casinos themselves.

I used to think my black leather coat and black Fedora-like hat were my superhero uniform that helped me bring in my power, but over the years my boss, Stan, the God of Poker, convinced me I was just being silly.

I still wore the black coat and black hat most of the time anyway, just like tonight. Made me feel better.

Patty Ledgerwood, aka Front Desk Girl, would be getting off work at the MGM Grand Hotel front desk in fifteen minutes. When I got done in a game ahead of her, instead of jumping to my office or to our condo to wait for her, I often just sat here in this perfectly comfortable chair and waited and enjoyed watching people.

That's how I managed to be in the right place at the right time to see a woman so starved and hungry, she could barely walk.

Wow, did she look out of place in the opulent richness of the MGM Grand.

She had long blonde hair that seemed to shimmer and her face was like that of a skeleton. She had on a white blouse, jeans, and a dress jacket that just hung on her frame.

No one in the moving crowds tended to pay her any attention at all, but my warning bells went off big time. This woman was in trouble and she flat didn't belong here.

As she neared me, I realized she only wore sandals that she could barely keep on her boney feet.

I took her and the rest of the area out of time. I loved that power of mine the most, outside of being able to teleport. I could slip between a moment of time, which made everyone around me just freeze. And the most startling thing about it was that all sound vanished as well.

Intense silence sometimes seemed louder than a casino full of gamblers and machines.

The extremely thin and clearly starving woman had green eyes that seemed far too large for her face and she was staring ahead as if not seeing anything.

My warning bells were going off big time, and I had no doubt I needed some help with this one.

"Stan?" I said into the air above me. "Could use a little advice on something."

Stan appeared beside me, also out of time. He had on his normal gray slacks, gray shirt and Cardigan button-down sweater. The guy could disappear in a crowd.

"What's the problem?"

I nodded to the thin blonde behind him.

He turned around and I thought he actually staggered a step forward. For the God of Poker to show any kind of emotion was almost unheard of.

"Ambrosia," he said softly, reverently.

"Laverne?" Stan said, glancing up as I had done when I called him. "Emergency."

I had no idea who this woman was and why it affected Stan so much. I did know from one of my lessons from Patty about the history of the gods that they called their food ambrosia in the early days. Made sense there would be a person with that name.

Laverne, Lady Luck herself, appeared. She was one of the most powerful gods on the planet and basically seemed to run everything. She had on her standard business power suit and her brown hair was pulled back tight, making her face look stark.

"Oh, no," she said, seeing Ambrosia. She moved over reverently to the skeletal woman, then looked at me. "Let's get her to your office."

I nodded and we all jumped away. I didn't care of the security cameras showed I just suddenly vanished. If anyone noticed, I would deal with it later.

As we jumped I sent a thought to Patty that we had an emergency and to meet in the office.

My office floated about a thousand feet above the Las Vegas Strip. It was invisible and was nothing more than a glass cube with a checkered tile floor. In the very center of the cube was a large diner booth that looked like it came right out of a 1950s diner with red vinyl seats and a Formica table-top.

There was a wood railing around the room at waist-high to stop the fear of falling off the floor, and there was a door in the back that connected to a small diner downtown near Fremont Street where Madge, a superhero in the food side of things and part of my team, worked. Anyone who couldn't teleport could come though the diner to get here.

As we arrived, Laverne had her arm around Ambrosia.

"This is fun," Ambrosia said, glancing around. Her voice was raspy and weak.

Then she looked at me. "You must be Poker Boy. I was hoping to meet you."

I bowed slightly and kept my mouth shut, something I had learned was always a good thing to do when you had no idea who you were meeting and how powerful they were.

From how Stan and Lorraine were reacting, Ambrosia must be very powerful, or very important in some way or another.

At that moment, Madge, the waitress from the diner came bursting into the office. I had never seen Madge in anything other than an old-style diner's waitress uniform two sizes too small for her figure. And I had never seen her upset or bothered at all. Now she was actually running.

"Mom," Madge said, hurrying to help Ambrosia sit in the booth.

I damned near choked.

Madge was crying.

Ambrosia hugged her.

And I was just about as lost as I had ever been, and that was going some.

Chapter Two

At that moment Patty arrived, still dressed in her front desk black and white MGM Grand uniform.

She gasped and then said in a whisper, "Ambrosia."

I was clearly in my normal state of cluelessness. But with Madge crying and Laverne working to get Ambrosia settled in the booth, now was clearly not the time for one of my really stupid questions.

I was still trying to get over the fact that this skeleton-thin woman was the mother of the large, oversized-in-many-ways superhero waitress that was part of my team.

Finally they got her settled, then Laverne looked at Madge. "Milkshakes."

Madge nodded, kissed Ambrosia gently on the head and

vanished. That was the first time I knew that Madge could actually teleport.

Stan slid into the booth across from Ambrosia and indicated that Patty and I join him.

Ambrosia's skin looked like it might crack and just fall off her bones and you could see blood vessels through it. She had clearly been a beautiful woman at one time.

Laverne sat with her arm around Ambrosia and no one spoke as Ambrosia seemed to nod off, only being held up by Laverne.

After only a moment or so Madge appeared with a vanilla milkshake for Ambrosia, one for Laverne, a chocolate one for Stan and a chocolate one for Patty and me to share.

Those had to be the fastest milkshakes ever made.

Laverne put the milkshake up close to Ambrosia and softly said, "Take a sip."

Madge hovered, watching.

Ambrosia nodded, leaned forward and took a sip.

It seemed as if the office glowed orange for a short moment.

Then Ambrosia took another sip and then another and I was right, the office was glowing a soft orange color.

And the skin on her face and arms seemed to become more healthy and as we watched, Ambrosia gained a good fifty pounds, fleshing out into the beautiful woman I had thought she could be, including her breasts that clearly were not originally small.

Wow, that was one powerful milkshake. Hell on any diet, that was for sure.

"Thank you, daughter. Laverne," Ambrosia said, nodding to Laverne and then looking up at Madge and smiling. "I have missed you both."

"I have missed you as well, Mom," Madge said.

Laverne just nodded and hugged Ambrosia.

"Can you tell us where you have been?" Laverne asked, moving slightly away to give Ambrosia more room to drink her milkshake.

With every sip, the once nearly-dead woman looked healthier.

I glanced at the milkshake in front of me and Patty and then scooted it toward her.

Patty just shook her head slightly. She clearly didn't want to gain fifty pounds and large breasts with a few sips either.

"I've been on our moon base," Ambrosia said.

I almost blurted out that I didn't know the gods had a moon base, but then managed to keep my mouth shut. Patty looked just as puzzled, so if she didn't know either, it would be no surprise I wouldn't know.

"You were there alone?" Laverne asked.

Ambrosia nodded, her long hair flowing in a golden river around her. "I wanted the peace and quite to get some calculations done."

"How did you get so thin?" Madge asked.

"Ran out of food a few decades back," Ambrosia said. "I didn't realize how bad I had gotten until I kept falling asleep in my lab. I barely had the energy to teleport back here. And everything here has changed so much, I didn't know what to do. I just hadn't been paying attention to the changes here on the planet."

My mouth finally worked faster than my brain. "So how did you know who I was?"

Ambrosia smiled at me and her green eyes seemed to see right through me. "You and this office and this town play a large part of the calculations I was doing, trying to work out some future events. My math told me you existed is all because you had to exist."

I just nodded. One of those times when the answer just confused me more.

"How long was I gone?" Ambrosia asked, glancing up at Madge.

"Just over two hundred years," Madge said. "We all missed you."

Ambrosia smiled and again the room seemed to light up with a soft orange glow.

"I missed you all as well," she said. "And it feels great to be back."

"Did you get the answers you were looking for?" Laverne asked.

Ambrosia shook her head. "No, I'm afraid I need to go back. Not quite done."

"Can I at least feed you regularly?" Madge asked.

Ambrosia smiled, again lighting up the room. "I would

love that. And we can catch up on what you have been doing for the last few centuries."

Madge just beamed. Clearly she loved her mother.

Ambrosia turned to Laverne. "And I would love to know what you have been doing as well."

There as a twinkle in Ambrosia's large green eyes and Laverne actually blushed.

"Besides feeding said," Laverne said, smoothly changing the subject, "is there anything we can do to help your project at this point?"

"No," Ambrosia said. "But as soon as there is, I will let you know."

Laverne pushed the untouched milkshake Madge had made her over in front of Ambrosia. "Grab that and you and I and Madge will go to my place and I'll cook us dinner."

Ambrosia smiled and moved to follow Laverne to stand. Then she looked at me and said, "Thank you for spotting me and helping me get here."

I again just bowed slightly.

And with that the three of them vanished, leaving me and Stan and Patty sitting in the booth a thousand feet above Las Vegas with untouched milkshakes.

"So who is Ambrosia exactly," I asked, looking at Stan.

"She is the god of formulas, mixtures, and recipes," Stan said. "And one of the most brilliant mathematicians to ever live."

"Moon base?" Patty asked.

Stan nodded. "Back in the days of the war with the giants,

before Atlantis, we had a moon base to stage attacks and to retreat to. After the war ended we maintained it for centuries, but as more new generations came along and all of us originals grew old and tired, it was mostly forgotten."

I just nodded. There were so many things I didn't know about the gods and superheroes.

"And what is the connection between Laverne and Ambrosia?" I asked.

"They were lovers before Ambrosia vanished," Stan said.

"Oh," I managed to say.

"I'll see you two later," Stan said. "Good work."

With that he vanished.

At least it hadn't been a total loss of a night. I had rescued an ancient god wondering the halls of the MGM Grand, starving. And I had learned that the gods had an ancient moon base.

And that milkshakes could make you gain a lot of weight and large boobs instantly. That was something I had always suspected, but tonight had confirmed.

I pointed to the two milkshakes. "You up for gaining some weight?"

Patty laughed. "Actually, I'm hungry and could use a good steak and salad."

Ten minutes later we were being seated in one of the best steak houses in the city. Another win for a very good night.

THE BIRTH OF A SUPERHERO

THE BIRTH OF A SUPERHERO

Janice Everly, aka "Ace," sat in the eighth spot at the table, right on the end, her back to the door. She didn't see me come into the poker room, which was probably for the better. But I had a hunch she sensed that I was here, even though she wouldn't know what she was sensing exactly.

I would have sensed that she was here, known someone of power was close.

She was dressed in a light sweatshirt of some type without writing on it and jeans and running shoes. She had a freshwater pearl necklace on top of the sweatshirt and matching earrings.

She looked in shape, like a runner. She had long brown hair that swept away from her face and back over her collar and bright green eyes that didn't miss much.

She was stunning, even dressed in a sweatshirt and jeans.

I had a hunch she didn't miss on a lot of men, either. Or women, if she went that way. She had classic good looks and a nice smile.

She wasn't in a hand, but was watching the play of two others at the end of the table. One was a local pro, a solid player, a grinder, who made enough money to live by playing low-stakes games for lots and lots of hours, basically earning minimum wage. The other guy was clearly a tourist, more than likely just stopping for a few hours on the way to the coast.

The grinder took his chips and Ace nodded to herself.

Five tables had games going on, pretty busy for a weekday afternoon in the Oregon Mountains. Spirit Winds Casino for the longest time had been my home casino. It had a mountain cabin feel to the decor, only with bright lights and slot machines.

Polished and huge log beams towered over the casino floor and fake pine trees sprouted at places in corners. The walls looked like they were pine boards with knots and everything, but on closer look it was just a fake tile of some sort. All the colors in the place were earth tones and greens, even the patterned carpet.

The poker room also had the mountain décor, only with lower ceilings, televisions on every wall, and comfortable brown leather chairs for the players. The felt on each table was a bright green, matching no color I had ever seen in nature.

The poker room was good-sized at twelve tables and in certain tournaments they used all twelve.

It was a good room, run by good people, but I just wasn't here much these days since I lived with my girlfriend Patty Ledgerwood in her condo in Vegas. However, we were building a massive home not far from here on twenty acres in the mountains. It had actually been under construction now for a good ten years and was looking wonderful.

Over the years the construction had just seemed to take on a life of its own and now was past ten thousand square feet with a massive pool and hot tub looking out over the mountain valley below. Patty and I planned on using it as a getaway, but nothing more. We both loved Vegas.

So building that monster might be the most stupid thing I had ever done, and with my history, that was saying something.

Last year Patty had finally gotten me to have hauled away and destroyed a double-wide old manufactured home. I used to live in it about a mile up the highway. Can't say I missed the place. But I lived there before I could teleport and since I was never home, it had served its purpose for my first years as a poker superhero.

I ate a lot of TV dinners in that place, let me tell you. I don't miss those, either.

Ace, as all her friends called her, and she had friends, which was a good sign, seemed to be a good person from what I had found out about her. Stan, my boss, friend, and the God of Poker, said she was a developing superhero in her early days. Ace didn't know that yet, either.

Took me years before Stan appeared one day and talked to me about the weird powers I seemed to be developing. Things like having almost a Spidey-sense for danger, being able to calm people down, being able to really read people and their emotions.

The teleportation and stopping time nifty powers wouldn't come for a few years. But those first few years sure were confusing up here in the mountains all on my own. I even used to think that my black coat and black fedora was my superhero costume and funneled the powers of a casino into me. Stan, bless his evil heart, let me go on thinking that for years.

So I was sent here by Stan to show Ace a few ropes. Basically to make contact, and I had not one idea how to do that.

Not one.

How do you tell someone, "Oh, by the way, your entire life is changing, you will get powers like you grew hair in puberty, and you will live maybe forever."

Yeah, easy.

But it did help that she happened to be in my old home casino. She actually lived in Seattle and was just doing some traveling and playing. I did a lot of that as well back in my early days. And banked everything and ended up so rich, I don't know what to do with it all. I had so many investments now, I needed a superhero accountant to keep track of it all.

So I figured to get to know another poker player, I should do what I do know how to do. I bought a rack of chips and sat down in the game three seats from her.

The dealer was an old guy named Gary and he smiled at me. "Great to see you back. Been awhile."

"Traveling too much," I said.

"How's the big house up on the hill coming?" Gary asked.

"Almost finished," I said.

Gary laughed. "Heard that before."

"Said it before," I said and laughed with Gary.

The entire time Ace watched me without really focusing on me. Nifty trick I had developed early in my poker career as well.

I tossed every hand for the next hour, kept my shields up so she couldn't sense anything from me, and watched Ace play. She was smart and left the grinder alone, but when she did play, it was clear she had a clear read on the tourist she was up against and she carved away steadily at their chip stacks.

She was good. And because she was so good-looking and friendly and smiled a lot, the tourists didn't even seem to notice they were getting plucked like so many chicken.

A few pointers and a little more practice and she could hold her own or win in any big game in Vegas. I was impressed.

I would have done what she did in almost exactly the same way.

And I knew for a fact my presence was driving her nuts.

Twice during the hour other employees of the room had stopped by to say hi. And that clearly bothered Ace more than she wanted to say.

I just kept glancing at my cards and tossing them. Not something any normal player would do in a fairly loose no-limit game.

My play or lack of play would have bothered me as well. As poker players, we want to be in control of the table we are at. I wasn't allowing that to happen for her. In fact, by buying in, being known by the room's staff, and then not playing, I had taken control without playing a hand.

So now the question was what was Ace going to do? I knew what I would do in her spot. Not play a hand against me if I did decide to play. And maybe just leave her chips to save her chair and head for dinner.

When you lose control, you stay out of the mix. That simple, but she was still young and my gut sense was that she would try to push me in some way.

I was wrong.

After another fifteen minutes, which she gained a good thousand into her stack of chips, she pushed back, told the dealer she would be back in ten or fifteen, and then left the room.

Stan might have found a good one this time. Looks like it was time to go introduce myself.

After a few more hands, I also left my chips and went in search of Ace. Didn't have to search hard. She was in the café and had a French Dip and fries in front of her.

The restaurant had the same mountain cabin feel as the rest of the casino, and in here the tables actually looked like they were carved out of logs and the chairs were polished wood.

The waiters and waitresses all wore Western-looking costumes that looked as fake as the rest of the place.

I took the entire restaurant and casino out of time except for Ace and me and walked up toward her.

She did a panicked look around as the lack of casino noise and movement became clear. I know at first, the lack of noise and everyone frozen can really mess with your mind. Especially the people all around her chewing with their mouths open. I actually didn't freeze time, I just took Ace and myself between an instant of time. But I called it freezing time because it felt that way.

I walked up toward her table as she looked like she either might be sick or would panic and sprint for the door.

"Nifty trick, huh?" I said.

She just looked at me blankly.

I extended my hand. "Everyone calls me Poker Boy. But that name is not known in that room or any room, actually."

She looked at my hand for a second, then shook it. "Ace."

"I know," I said, sitting down and taking one of her fries. "I came here tonight to introduce myself and you into your future."

"What the hell is happening?" she asked.

"I slipped us between a moment in time is all," I said.

"Numbers of years down the road you might learn how to do that."

She just looked around, shaking her head.

"Hang on," I said. "I'll put us back in the flow so all these people can keep chewing, but I got to go back to where I was so the cameras don't notice anything."

I stood up, went back to near the hostess station and let the noise and the sounds of the casino come crashing back in. Then I retraced my steps to her table and sat back down.

"That better?" I asked.

"If you want me to pay attention to what the hell you are saying, yes."

I laughed and took another fry. "Don't remember these being that good here."

"So what the hell are you?" she asked. "I could sense something different about you, but then when you sat down, you blocked it somehow."

"That's one of your powers starting to develop," I said.

"Powers?"

"Yup, at your age, you are starting to develop powers that will get stronger and more refined as you practice them and get a little older. Can you feel when you are in danger, or when a hand is a loser?"

She slowly nodded.

"Can you sense when something is going wrong? Or if someone is really evil?"

She nodded slowly once again, her eyes wide.

"I know how you are feeling right now," I said. "Not a power, but because I have been in your shoes. When my boss, Stan the God of Poker told me this stuff, I thought he was totally full of shit, other than the fact that he was right."

"God of Poker?" Ace asked.

"Yup," I said, nabbing another of her fries. I was sure after this she wasn't going to be eating much. "I work for him, technically, as a superhero in the world of poker. That's what you are developing into, a superhero. You also will work for Stan. He has a lot of us around the world, since poker is so popular."

Ace opened her mouth, than shut it, her eyes sort of glazed. Didn't blame her for an instant.

"Think of it this way," I said. "Every aspect of our life and the world has a god and superheroes involved in it. You develop these powers naturally as you hit a certain age."

"Seriously?" she asked.

I nodded. "There are gods for every little thing, and super-heroes working for them. For example, my girlfriend and love of my life is named Patty and she's a superhero in the world of hospitality. She works right now on the front desk at the MGM Grand in Vegas. She has the ability to calm down the most angry person imaginable. And a bunch of other stuff as well, some of which I am sure she hasn't shown me yet."

I decided not to tell her that Patty was a good thousand years, maybe more, older than I was. Poor kid was having to soak in enough.

"So what do superheroes do in poker?" she asked.

"I remember asking Stan that same question," I said. "Basically our job is to help people. Save people, often from themselves. And play poker. I know, tough life, but someone has to do it."

She actually smiled at that. I was going to like this kid if she laughed at my humor.

"So what do I do now?" she asked.

"Besides eating your sandwich before I eat all your fries?" I asked.

She nodded.

"You start focusing on your powers, see what they are, experiment a little with them to learn them," I said.

She nodded.

"And become a better poker player."

"Been working on that," she said.

"And if you need help or have questions, you do what I do. You look up at the ceiling and say, 'Stan?'"

She frowned. "Why look at the ceiling?"

"Damned if I know," I said. "I always figured it was because he was a god. And remember when you meet other gods, which you will, always be polite and bow a lot. Remember, they are actually gods."

She nodded, now looking very worried.

"Let me introduce you to your boss," I said. "Remember where your hands and arms are. He's going to come in out of time."

Ace nodded and I looked up at the wood beam above me and said, "Stan?"

All the sounds of the restaurant and the casino beyond vanished as Stan appeared, dressed in his normal tan slacks, tan shirt, tan button-down sweater. The guy was so plain he could vanish in a crowd of two people.

Ace stood and bowed.

Stan actually smiled and moved to shake Ace's hand while I nabbed another fry.

"Poker Boy here get you all screwed up?" Stan asked.

"I don't think so, sir," Ace said, bowing slightly once again.

"Oh, he will," Stan said. "Give him time."

"Thanks for the vote of confidence, boss," I said.

Stan gave me a dirty look and then said to Ace. "You don't need to bow or call me sir."

"But doesn't hurt with some of the other gods," I said.

With that Stan nodded. "To get me, all you need to do was what Poker Boy just did. Any question or problem, don't hesitate, understand?"

Ace nodded.

"Now sit down," Stan said. "I got a date to get back to."

With that I almost went over backwards in my chair. Stan? Date? I doubt he had been with a woman since his wife died in Atlantis.

"Date?"

"With my daughters," Stan said, smiling at me.

He did that to me on purpose.

Then he looked at Ace. "Any time, remember? I am always available."

Then as we got back into the positions that we were in before he showed up, he vanished and the sound of the casino came crushing back in.

"Can you teleport like that?" Ace asked.

"I can and it's great fun and saves a ton on gas and airline fees," I said. "Given time you will learn that too."

She just sort of nodded.

"Think you can focus enough on cards to take some of my money?" I asked, turning the conversation back to what she knew the best.

She nodded. "Give me fifteen minutes to get my shit together and eat and I'll be back."

I nodded and reached across the table and shook her hand as I stood. "Remember, don't call me Poker Boy at any table."

"Copy that," she said.

"And I am not your boss, just your friend. So feel free to ask me questions as well, but you will have to find me. I have no idea how Stan does that 'can hear you from anywhere' thing."

Ace laughed and seemed to relax a little as I turned and headed back for the poker room.

I had played about five or six hands by the time she got back and sat down.

She nodded to me and then checked her chips.

She felt completely different than before. Now I felt a

power radiating from her and it looked like her brain was back behind those green eyes.

And by the time all the tourists waiting to join our table faded off into the morning hours, both of us had very, very large stacks of chips. And I have to admit, I didn't have many of hers and she didn't have many of mine.

It was the most fun poker game I had played in a very long time.

Age Might Be A
Number

Age Might Be a Number

"Got an old friend coming for lunch," Patty said as we stood in my office looking out over the city of Las Vegas and the Strip below us.

I have no idea why I got a shudder, but I did. Not from the word friend, but from the word "old" modifying friend. I had no idea how old Patty really was, but got a hunch I might find out today.

We had made it a habit to get to my invisible floating office about fifteen minutes before anyone else arrived, just to stand and look at the city together, talk about our mornings, take a break from everyone else.

I loved that time, to be honest.

Patty said she did as well.

The day outside of my Vegas office was a hot one, and the

air was shimmering from the heat. I never noticed the hot days or the few days in the winter when it got actually cold. I seldom was outside. And since I could teleport everywhere, I had no need to even get in a car.

Sometimes being a superhero had its real advantages.

Another was having an invisible floating platform encased in four glass walls and a glass ceiling a thousand feet in the air with a 1950s diner booth as the only furniture besides a few chairs. I loved my office and so did a lot of other superheroes and gods. Just never knew who was going to show up for lunch.

"How long has it been since you have seen her?" I asked.

"A very long time," Patty said, smiling at me.

Maybe I wasn't going to find out how old my girlfriend was after all.

"What's her name?" I asked.

"Iris," Patty said. "She's a god that works in the area of weather."

"Cool," I said.

"And really hot," a voice from behind us said.

Both Patty and I spun around to see one of the most beautiful woman I have ever seen. And she seemed to be glowing with rainbows of colors. I had never seen that before. It was like her aura was just blowing away from her body. Only sparkly. Never seen a sparkly aura, either.

She stood about Patty's height at five-five and wore jeans, running shoes, and a decorative blouse. She had long blond hair down over her shoulders and a smile that lit up my office like it was the inside of a lighthouse.

"Iris!" Patty almost screamed like a teenaged girl.

"Patty!" Iris also almost screamed.

And an instant later they were hugging each other.

And all the rainbow of colors just surrounded them like a light show.

Wow, it really had been a long time.

Finally, they broke the hug and just stared into each other's eyes for a very long moment, both their smiles so wide, I thought it might hurt their faces.

Then Patty said, "This is Poker Boy."

She indicated me.

Then she added something that almost made me melt into the tile floor of my office. She said, "The love of my life."

The god named Iris turned to me and bowed slightly and offered her hand, which I shook, hoping all the rainbow stuff didn't stick to me too badly.

"Anyone who can capture Patty's heart is a friend of mine."

"Thank you," I said. "Wonderful to meet you."

"And wow, this is an amazing office," Iris said as she slowly turned around and took in the view.

At that moment things got even wilder. Stan, the God of Poker, showed up and when he saw Iris, he broke into a huge smile, something I had almost never seen him do.

And they hugged.

Stan actually hugged someone and seemed to really enjoy it. What was it about this woman?

Then in short order, Iris got hugs from a very happy Madge and a very happy Ben as they appeared.

Everyone was glad to see Iris, they all clearly liked her a lot, and it was clear she had been gone a very long time.

Madge got everyone's order and left, than Patty and Iris slid into the booth beside me. Stan and Ben sat across from us like normal.

Patty and Iris were like two high school girls, giggling and laughing and basically keeping us all entertained. Right up to the moment that Lady Luck, Laverne appeared.

She pulled a chair over and sat down at the end of the table like she always did for lunch.

She was not smiling.

Oh, oh…

Patty and Iris went silent, as did Ben and Stan, and all smiles vanished. Iris lost all the rainbow stuff that had been sort of just flowing from her the entire time.

"Iris," Laverne said.

"Hera," Iris said, bowing slightly with her head.

Now I knew Laverne had been married to Zeus, but I did not know she had been Hera. Holy shit, no wonder she scared me all the time.

"I go by Laverne these days."

Iris nodded.

"How have things been in Australia?" Laverne asked.

"It's a good place to live," Iris said. "But my work is stuck at the moment."

"Global warming?" Laverne asked.

Iris nodded. "The technology here is like trying to stop a runaway car with a pillow. That's why I came here today, to see everyone and ask a favor."

"Honestly," Laverne said. "I'm glad you did. You and I should have cleared the air long ago."

"I wanted to," Iris said.

"So did I," Laverne said, extending her hand toward Iris, palm up.

Iris and Patty both looked like they might cry, then Iris put her hand in Laverne's hand and they sat there for a moment.

It felt like a massive weight was lifted from the room. Wow. I just hoped at some time in the future, someone would explain to me what had happened between the two way back in the past. But even though I am known for asking stupid questions, I also know when the time is wrong for any question.

Finally, Laverne pulled her hand back and, smiling, said, "What can we do to help?"

"I need to return to Olympus with a few of my assistants," Iris said.

"For the computers?" Laverne asked.

Iris nodded. "If we're going to find a way to slow down this coming disaster, I'm going to need them."

"Of course," Laverne said. "It's your home, you can

return back at any time. Just keep me updated on the progress."

"Thank you, Chairman," Iris said, smiling.

"Laverne," Lady Luck said. "Just Laverne for now."

Then suddenly the fun was back at the table and shortly Madge brought up the fantastic burgers and fries and milkshakes.

I said nothing, just sat there and ate and listened, trying to get hints from the conversations with Iris and Patty and Laverne and Ben about how old Patty really was.

I got a few, maybe just enough to ask Patty a few questions later.

Finally, as we were finishing, Iris asked, "Does he ever talk?"

She indicated me.

I didn't think the table would stop laughing. I was sure they could hear us down on the Strip over the traffic noise.

I think Stan, my boss, laughed the hardest.

"He's just trying to figure out how old I am," Patty said. "He's only been a superhero for about twenty years, so I haven't told him yet."

"Ego?" Iris asked, pretending to stare at me, but I could tell she was trying not to smile.

"Just a game," Patty said, smiling at me and then winking.

"You children," Iris said, shaking her head.

"They are cute most of the time," Ben said, and Stan and Laverne just nodded and smiled.

"But from what I hear," Iris said, "you all have saved the entire world a few times."

"More than a few," Laverne said.

All I could do was smile at that. So they all thought Patty was young as well.

"So tell me," I said, finally breaking my silence with my first question of the day. "How did you two meet?"

Iris looked at Patty and smiled. "What was it? 1870 in Chicago?"

"1871," Patty said. "I bought the house from a client and you came to work for me."

"Rough, but fun year," Iris said. "We had some good clients, if I remember? The mayor and everyone. Right up to the day the house burnt down in the great fire."

"At least we got all the girls out safely," Patty said.

I glanced at Stan and even with the best poker face on the planet, he was having a hard time not laughing.

They were pulling my leg.

Laverne just laughed and stood and with one more fry in her hand said to Patty, "At some point you'll need to tell him. Good luck with the research, Iris."

With that she vanished and Patty and Iris were just laughing, again, like high school girls. Amazing they didn't have phones in their hands texting at the same time.

"Good luck," Ben said to me, laughing, then he vanished.

Stan just shook his head and vanished as well, leaving me with two giggling women.

"I got a tournament at the Bellagio," I said. "I think I'll give you two time to catch up."

"When will your tournament be over?" Patty asked.

"About five if I make it the entire way," I said.

"Dinner at the steakhouse there at five," Patty said. "The three of us and I promise I'll tell you honestly how we met and how old I really am."

"Sounds super," I said.

Patty leaned over and kissed me. Then she said, "You are my one true love, just remember that."

Then holding hands, the two laughing women jumped away, leaving me sitting in my own office with a table of left-over burger baskets and a bunch of uneaten fries.

And a deep-down worry that maybe ending the game of guessing Patty's age was a game I didn't want to really end.

But at the same time I did.

I won the tournament and it turned out that my guess about Patty was right all along, that she was about a hundred years older than me, which also made her very young in this superhero and gods world.

She was born in 1891 in New York and became a super-hero around 1920. She and Iris met by accident and Iris helped Patty escape a bad, abusive marriage, which is why Patty didn't like to talk about her early years and we had never talked about marriage.

The two of them remained very close until Iris headed to Australia to live in 1940 for the Second World War. They were like sisters, even though Iris was an original god who fought the Giants and had lived in Atlantis and came down from Olympus.

It became clear to me, even with my thick skull, that age among gods and superheroes made no difference at all. Just none.

And it certainly didn't with me and Patty. Not in the slightest.

And honestly, I ended up laughing with the women all through that dinner. Not quite giggling, but certainly having a great time.

GHOSTS OF POKER GAMES PAST

CHAPTER ONE

Someday I will learn that when I think I am having an uneventful night, it never turns out that way. Just flat never.

My night started at the Golden Nugget poker room in downtown Las Vegas. I hadn't visited that room for maybe six months, but it was a good room and I sort of felt, as Poker Boy, a superhero of poker, I should visit all the poker rooms in Vegas at least a couple times a year. And all the ones in California, Oregon, and Nevada at least once a year. Some nights I jumped from two or three of the small rooms, spending an hour in each.

The Golden Nugget room held eighteen tables and three times a day had some sort of tournament going on three of those tables. It had a low ceiling, like most older hotel poker rooms, and was decorated in dark mahogany, with a dark carpet and lighter textured wallpaper between the mahogany columns.

I liked the place. It just felt good.

When the room was crowded, as it was on this Thursday, it took some squeezing around chairs and other players to get to a table along the inside wall. Part of the charm is how I figured it. I spent a lot of time elbow to elbow with other poker players. Being crowded was just part of the game.

I had found a very nice 5-10 no-limit game, and was enjoying taking the tourists' money while pretending everything I was doing was luck. People said I was fun to play with, and I tried to play up that image. It certainly helped my bank accounts.

I planned on being here until my girlfriend Patty got off work at ten from the MGM Grand front desk. We had a late dinner planned at a new place in the Resorts World Hotel and Casino that we had been hearing about and I was looking forward to meal and the time with Patty.

I was about to fold a two-three not-suited when suddenly I found myself in a very different room.

Maybe four tables, lots and lots of smoke in the air and the five at the table with me were all smoking, one a very nasty-smelling cigar. There hadn't been smoking in poker rooms since the turn of the century.

I glanced down at the chips I had in front of me that were larger than normal chips just slightly, and I had them racked in a wooden rack and sitting in front of me.

Everyone had their chips in a wooden rack as well. Just

how it was done in a certain time in history, but not in modern poker. Racks were all plastic and only used to carry chips to and from a table. Racks were not allowed on a table.

And everyone around me and in the rest of the four-table room was dressed in old-fashioned suits, with ties and all.

I had started off the night in my black leather coat, a silk shirt under it, and jeans. Now I wore a black suit, a Fedora black hat, and a black tie. All matched perfectly over a white shirt that felt suddenly like it had a little too much starch in certain places.

I took a deep breath to calm my heart. I didn't have a sense of immediate danger, and the tables of poker just all looked normal.

My table was playing Seven Card Stud, a game I was pretty good at, but hadn't played in years, since it was pretty much out of fashion in 2022.

Then I noticed the heat.

Stifling heat.

I could see a lot of very old-fashioned slot machines in rows between the poker room and the wide-open doors leading out to the street.

Numbers of men, almost all men in fact, sat at those machines, pulling the arm on the machine to make the wheels spin.

The only women in the place were two well-built women with low-cut blouses and short skirts with nylons and high heels carrying a large wooden tray of cigars and cigarettes.

And everyone around me was sweating as a number of

large fans in the corners blew the smoke around, but did little to drop the temperature.

Outside it was clearly early evening, and a lot of very large cars were going by, and couples strolling on the sidewalks.

The bet of 25 cents was to me and I folded my cards, even though it was clear I had a pretty good hand.

I picked up the wooden rack of chips and headed for what looked to be a cashier's cage just outside the room.

I cashed in for one-hundred-and-twenty-seven dollars, shoved the money in my otherwise empty pockets, and went out on the sidewalk.

I recognized instantly where I was at.

Fremont Street in downtown Las Vegas.

I had been playing in the old poker room in the Golden Gate. Those poker tables in there hadn't lasted more than a few years.

The train station was still at the end the street on my left and a few other old casinos I had seen in pictures were stretched along the street to my right.

"Before 1951," I said softly to myself, since the Plaza Hotel and Casino had replaced the train station at that point. But I knew this wasn't much before that point. This did not look like war pictures of this city.

What in the world had happened?

Who had brought me here and why?

I had been yanked back in the past once before and had not enjoyed it. This time around I was managing to keep the panic under control for the moment, but there was no doubt

I needed help. I knew nothing about time travel, even though I had met Father Time. All I knew was that the gods and superheroes all feared time travel for the problems it could cause.

I moved around the corner onto Main Street, which was not as full of people as Fremont, and got to a place I could take myself out of time. That was a fun skill I had developed that allowed me to step between an instant in time, making everyone around me seem to freeze.

All the sounds of the night, the car horns, the engines, the slot machines bells coming from open casino doors, vanished.

"Stan of 2022," I said, looking up at the sky slightly. "Need a little help?"

The last time I had been here, I had called for Stan and ended up trying to explain to Stan, the God of Poker, that I worked for him in the future. Had not been fun.

"What the hell?" Stan said as he appeared inside my bubble and looked around.

This was my Stan, dressed in tan slacks, a tan sweater over a white shirt, and loafers. In 2022 he could blend into any crowd and just vanish. Here, in this time, he would stand out like a flashing sign.

"You tell me?" I said, sort of indicating the older cars and the old train station where the Plaza Hotel was supposed to be. "I was playing in a great game in the Nugget when I suddenly found myself dressed like this, in a game in the old Golden Gate, or whatever it is called at this point in time."

"It's October, 1950," Stan said. "And you look good. Sort of evil, but good."

"Thanks," I said. "I think."

Stan looked around, clearly puzzled. "There are very few gods who can travel in time. So I'm going to go talk with Laverne and figure out why this is going on. I will be back. Don't mess up any timelines while I am gone."

And he vanished.

And for the moment I decided to just stand there, out of time, with everything around me frozen, trying to get my heartbeat down to just racing speed.

CHAPTER TWO

Stan showed up with Laverne in under a minute, but since this was time travel, for all I knew a few months had passed back in the present while they figured this out. More than likely not, but as little as I knew about time travel, anything was possible.

Laverne had on her standard business suit with her long brown hair pulled back tight off her head, making her look even more stern than normal. She glanced around for an instant, then said, "Well, damn."

Now I have worked with Laverne, Lady Luck herself, numbers of times, and every time, without fail, that I heard her swear, things were not good.

"Just ahead of the gate, huh?" Stan said.

Laverne nodded and I just stood there, clueless. Typical for me in the presence of two gods.

"Someone is trying to alter the fixed-point," Laverne said.

"What do they have against Las Vegas?" Stan asked, shaking his head.

"Explanation, please?" I said.

"In about two hours," Stan said, "at that table you were at, a fight breaks out between a cheater and two others at the table. Two are killed and the fight sparks a fire that destroys this entire block of the city, killing hundreds more."

"I don't remember anything about that," I said.

"Because it happened in another timeline," Laverne said. "In that timeline the fight and the fire gave Las Vegas the reputation of being dangerous, since entire families were killed in the fire. And the fact that it is becoming a mob town didn't help. So tourists stayed away and eventually the town became nothing more than a stop on the highway between Utah and California."

"Train station stayed right there," Stan said, "and the mob casinos out on the strip were shut down and finally torn down. Half of the buildings on this street are abandoned or torn down or burnt down and they call Las Vegas mostly a ghost town in 2022 in that timeline."

"Holy shit," I said, trying to imagine the vibrant, alive city that I knew and loved ending up like that.

"So how did you stop it the first time?"

"I sat in the game," Stan said. "Spotted the cheater and got him out of the game before anyone else figured out what he was doing and the fight could get started. I still have a very clear memory of that."

"So is something going to happen to you?" I asked.

Stan shook his head. "I just joined that game now, taking the seat you must have left. My memory remains the same. I'll have the cheater out of the casino and into the street in about thirty minutes."

This was not making any sense at all. "If that is the case, why am I here? And who brought me back through time?"

"This is a fixed point in time," Laverne said. "The event at that table changes everything about this town. And a lot of other events into the future as well. Please stay inside this time bubble and let me talk to Chronos and a few others who might know what is happening and why."

"Take your time," I said.

She wasn't smiling when she vanished.

"Good luck," Stan said. "I can't help you, I'm afraid."

And with that he vanished as well.

So I just stood there on Main Street of Las Vegas in October, 1950, in a time bubble so nothing was moving around me.

Sometimes, as a superhero, things just got weird. But I had to admit, there was no getting used to this level of complete weirdness.

CHAPTER THREE

Since no time was moving around me, it felt much longer than the actual three minutes it took for Laverne to return. She didn't look happy. Lady Luck not looking happy always sent chills up my spine. After all, I was a poker player.

"It seems," she said, "that from the time historians that I have talked to, Stan didn't clear up the major fixed-point in time by just getting the cheater out of the equation. He just delayed it."

"Stopping the fight wasn't enough?" I asked.

She shook her head. "This time around we have to stop and remove the fighters," Laverne said. "Time itself is like a river and it always finds a way. Now the only way to really cure this fixed-point in time, change the course of time and set it into the path to the future, is to let the fight start."

"And stop it before people die?" I asked. "And the place burns down?"

"Exactly," Laverne said.

"Can't Stan in there just let it keep going?"

"No," Laverne said. "The Time Board brought you back here to continue what Stan started."

"There is a Time Board?" I asked. I thought over the last decade I had learned a lot about superheroes and the gods. Seems I had missed something. More than likely a lot of somethings.

"The Time Board very seldom acts," she said. "But they need you now to take this point in time and change the flow. Missing will not only destroy Las Vegas, but it seems there are a few world wars that will happen as well."

No pressure was what I wanted to say.

Instead, I managed to take a deep breath and then said, "Well, people do love their gambling."

Laverne, ever serious, since she is Lady Luck, just shook her head and went on.

"As soon as the Stan of this time gets the cheater out into the street, you need to go in and take one of their seats at that table."

"Then what do I do?"

"Cheat," Lady Luck said. "And after a time, let them catch you."

"Cheat?" Not sure, but I think my voice squeaked like I was a teenager asking a girl out on a date.

She nodded. "We want you to cheat and make sure they

catch you. And the moment one of the men at the table goes for his gun inside his coat, freeze time before he shoots you."

"Now that's a plan," I said, managing to keep my normal voice and level for the full affect of the sarcasm.

"A representative of the Time Board and I will jump in, take over the bubble, and make sure the time line flows the way it needs to flow."

I nodded. "I'm going to be using time bubbles to help myself cheat, so don't jump the gun, so to speak."

"Call me when the moment comes," she said.

I thought for a moment Lady Luck might wish me good luck, but instead she just vanished.

I let myself take a few deep breaths before dropping the time bubble around me and letting in the noise of a busy night in 1950 Las Vegas.

Chapter Four

I went across Main Street and to the platform of the train station where I could see the front door of the Golden Gate Casino. Farther up Fremont Street were two other smaller gaming places and then the Golden Nugget. Beyond that the Four Queens. All of them had their doors open.

On the other side of Fremont was two smaller casinos and then the Apache Club. Beyond that the Fremont Casino.

The street was full of large sedans, the kind with vinyl slick seats that with every corner you could slide around inside like a pinball bouncing off bumpers.

If I knew cars, old classic cars, I bet I would be really enjoying this moment, but I didn't know a make or model or year of any of them. All I knew was that this point in time was a very few short years from the end of World War II.

And somehow those monster cars managed to not bump into each other or any of the pedestrians just crossing the street at will, mostly half drunk.

All the men were dressed like I was, suit, vest, slacks, matching plain tie, and white shirts. My black shoes were dusty, even though both Main Street and Fremont Street were paved.

The only women to be seen were hanging onto men's arms.

And the street was well-lit but not like it would be over the next seventy years.

I really wanted to ditch the jacket and vest in the heat, but no one else was, so I just stood there and sweated until Stan finally brought a guy out of the Golden Gate and turned up the street away from me.

Within a minute I was back in the Golden Gate and asking for a chair in at the table Stan and the cheater had just left.

I handed one of the two in charge of the room the money in my pocket and he brought me a wooden rack of chips that I sat in front of me.

Seems as if the two fighters were to my left. They both wore suits similar to mine. Dark cloth, dark hats, dark ties. The one closest to me had a scar across his cheek and both looked a lot like mod, or what I imagined a mod guy would look like in 1950.

The room was still filled with smoke and the two women with low cut blouses and carrying big trays were doing their best to keep the cigarettes and cigars flowing and lit.

Seven Card Stud is played with first dealing each player two cards down and one card up. Then we bet.

After that three more up cards, each one a betting round, then the last card was down.

Both my first two hands looked horrible, but I bet one and called the second all the way to the last card, letting the other four at the table know I was here to play and not real bright.

I lost both hands.

Next hand I did the same, only this time I cheated, stopping time and making my hand better. I did that for the next four hands, seeming to win all four just out of the blue.

And the two beside me were getting angry, I could sense it. The one guy closest to me just kept stroking the scar on his cheek which I took to mean as a threat. And to be honest, it was threatening.

So the next hand I waited to stop time until one of them had looked at their two down cards, then I took the best one and put it in my hand.

I heard mumbling after that hand of cheating, so the next hand I let the guy with the scar see me pull a card from my sleeve.

He shoved back from the table, knocking his chair into the fan against the wall, and shouted "Cheater!"

With that, his hand went into his coat and the guy beside him stood and did the same.

My heart was beating about as fast as I had ever felt it beat.

I froze time, then shouted "Laverne!"

The guy with the scar had his gun out of his jacket, the other guy wasn't far behind. Both guns looked nasty. I hated anything to do with guns.

Laverne appeared beside me, along with a guy dressed in green slacks, a white golf shirt, and a golf glove on his left hand.

"Is the timing right?" Laverne asked golfer guy.

"Perfect," the golf guy said. He pointed to the chair knocking the old electrical fan over. "Fire sparks from there. These two mob boys kill both Poker Boy here and the dealer and wound about five others, including one of the cigar girls. Six others in here have guns and the entire thing breaks out into the street where a young child is wounded and his father killed."

"Can we take care of it?" Laverne asked.

The golf guy moved over to the fan and unplugged it, sat it upright and then looked around. "We can."

Somehow, I managed to just stand there and watch and not even say anything stupid.

Laverne turned to me and said, "Thank you once again, Poker Boy. Patty is waiting for you."

The guy in the golf outfit nodded as well and the next moment I was back in my office floating over Las Vegas.

And Patty was there.

She grabbed me and hugged me and then kissed me.

"You're alive and back here," she said, holding me at arm's length. "So I assume it worked."

"Laverne and some guy in golf clothes from the Time Board seem to think it did."

"Time Board?" Patty asked.

"Yeah, that's what I said."

I sure like the new duds," she said. "Brings back great memories."

I glanced down at the black suit, black tie, black vest, black slacks, and pure white, over-starched shirt. I also still had on the black Fedora.

"You want to help me out of them?" I asked. "No real air-conditioning back in those days."

"I remember," she said.

"You in Vegas at that time?" I asked. I knew she was at least that old, but no idea how old she really was.

"I was," she said, rubbing up against me as her uniform from the MGM Grand changed into a low-cut cigarette girl outfit with the Golden Gate logo on it.

"What?" I asked.

"I thought you were so handsome back then. I just stared at you all the time you were in there until you suddenly vanished. I wanted to help you out of that suit then. Been waiting seventy-two years for this fantasy to come true."

With that we went instantly from my office to our bedroom in Patty's apartment and she pushed me back on the bed and began peeling off the cigar girl costume as I sat there and watched until she was totally naked.

And then she stood me up, tossed my hat onto the bed, and slowly, oh, so slowly, worked to untie my tie.

That took an amazingly long time to do between kisses, but as I had learned tonight, time was very relative.

And the buttons on my vest took even longer.

Or it sure seemed that way. And I loved every moment of it.

The Fun Starts Here

Just Turn The Page...

SNEAK PEEK

BEING DEAD (THE FIRST YEAR)

Chapter One

Dying on a first date sucks.

Dying on a blind date sucks even worse.

Especially when your date dies with you. And then goes off through some tunnel of light into the next life or something, leaving you sitting alone, dead, in a dark alley, waiting for your own tunnel of light.

Hands down, the worst ending to any date in recorded history.

The alley we had been forced to go into was blacker than the inside of a latrine, and seeing how it smelled, I would have not been surprised to be in a latrine, but I knew I wasn't since it seemed that being dead meant I could see just fine in the dark.

And smell just fine as well. Holy crap. The nearby Chinese restaurant garbage smelled like my fridge after six days of feeling sorry for myself and laying on the couch and eating take-out without taking out the uneaten food in the original cartons. And no telling how many homeless and drunks had actually used this alley for a bathroom.

I was sitting on a big green dumpster owned by a nearby office, so thankfully it didn't have the odor of the other dumpsters coming up between my legs.

The scum with the greasy black hair and dirty ski parka that had killed us was going through my date's pockets as I sat and watched.

The guy looked skinny and no doubt drug-addicted. His motions were jerky, his eyes darting around him like a rat trying to find a way out of a maze.

My blind date, dear old Handsome Bob, as I had started to think of him for the full thirty minutes I had known him, had caused this mess by thinking he could be a macho asshole or something.

The scum with the greasy black hair had approached us on the sidewalk and Bob had shaken his head and said, "Not now."

We were headed down the street to a nice Italian restaurant that served the best red wine and bread plate this side of New York. And that was going some for the Old Towne section of Boise, Idaho.

Bob was dressed in a clearly expensive silk suit and no tie, while I didn't look so cheap myself. For the date I had put on dark slacks, a white silk blouse with pearls around my neck, and a thin see-through sweater. No bra because I wanted my date to get an occasional peek at what might be offered after dinner if things went right.

Sitting dead in an alley sure wasn't my idea of things going right.

The greasy jerk had pulled out a gun, his hands shaking. Dear old dead Handsome Bob had said, "You don't want to do that."

Bless him.

Clearly the druggie did want to do exactly what he was doing, but I didn't say that. I was busy ramping up one of my super powers.

You see, before I was so suddenly cut down, I had worked as a superhero in the housing and hotel industry. Over the last century I had worked both front desks of hotels and sold real estate. At the moment I was on the real estate side, trying to help out in the booming Boise real estate market.

Amazing the kind of crap that goes on in real estate when big money is involved.

I hit greasy-hair with a full dose of my calming power. The guy was so high on drugs my power actually didn't do anything but make him stop shaking so hard.

He pointed to the dark alley with the gun. "Get in there and then dig out your money."

"And if we say no?" Handsome Bob asked the guy.

Since Bob was almost a foot taller than the greasy-haired druggie, I suppose Bob thought he could bully the situation a little.

Bless dear old now-dead stupid Bob.

I hit the guy with another dose of calming power. I had enough power on a normal day to stop a shouting, irate, pissed-off hotel customer at a front desk and make them smile.

The guy with the gun got calmer, but his pea brain was still set on robbing us. At least I got him to not shoot us right there on the sidewalk because of Handsome Bob's stupidity.

"Let's just give him our stuff and he will let us go," I said to Bob.

"Smart woman," the guy said, smiling and showing a mouthful of rotted teeth.

Actually, I had planned that when we got into the alley I would simply jump us away from this nut and then figure out something to tell dear old Bob.

Bob didn't know I was a one-hundred-year-old superhero and could just teleport anywhere I wanted. Not something you tell someone before a first blind date. Men tended to have sexual problems when they realized the woman they were with was over a hundred.

Bob nodded to me and we walked the twenty steps into the alley, Bob pushing me slightly ahead of him.

Then, as we stopped and turned at just about the point where the rotted Chinese food odor got the worst, Bob went to lunge at the guy.

Handsome Bob went to really, really stupid Bob very quickly.

I was so surprised Bob would do something that idiotic, I didn't react fast enough to jump us out of there.

The guy fired, hitting Bob in the arm.

The bullet went through Bob's flesh and hit me square between the eyes.

Now that was a shocker, let me tell you.

One moment I am standing alive in the alley and the next I am a ghost sitting on a smelly dumpster watching dear old Handsome Bob hold his arm and swear.

The greasy-haired guy was now twitching again. He stared at my body lying there in the alley, clearly getting my wonderful blouse and sweater all stained up with my own blood.

Then he looked at Bob, who was also staring at me, holding his wounded arm and looking sick to his stomach.

Then the guy did what any self-respecting murderer would do. He shot Bob.

Bob slumped to the ground and the guy fired one more shot into Bob's head.

A moment later I watched Bob's ghost stand up, look around, then look up and float off into a white light.

"Nice meeting you jerk-face," I shouted after Bob.

I was pretty sure he didn't hear me.

As I said, the worst ending to a blind date ever.

CHAPTER TWO

The druggie who had killed me and my blind date started through Bob's pockets. The druggie pulled out a money clip and then took Bob's watch. Then he rolled Bob over slightly and took out his wallet.

He pulled out a single-package condom and tossed it aside.

I just shook my head. "Damn, Bob, only one? Where was the confidence? If you had come back to my place, you would have needed at least three just to make it to breakfast."

The greasy murderer clearly didn't hear me. And I had a hunch dead Bob didn't either.

I glanced around. I was still the only ghost in the alley.

Where was my greeting party?

I figured I had become a Ghost Agent, which was why I hadn't gotten the beam-of-light ride. I had never met a Ghost

Agent, but I had heard from my best friend Patty that she and her boyfriend, Poker Boy, had worked with some Ghost Agents just lately to save the world. Seems Patty and her boyfriend were always saving the world, which I must admit I appreciated.

The guy stood and stepped toward my body.

"Hey, not so fast there, jerk-face," I said, jumping down from the dumpster and brushing off my pants.

The greasy-haired slime-ball picked up my clutch purse and went through it. That I didn't much care about. I had a few hundred in there and that was that.

But then he looked around at the mouth of the alley and then looked back at me with that look I had seen scum like him get. Ghost or no ghost, he wasn't touching me, even if I did have a hole in the middle of my forehead.

This night had gone bad enough as it was.

The guy kneeled down beside my body and I took two quick steps at the guy and went to kick him clear across the alley.

Foot went right through him. Charlie Brown would have been proud of my form, though. I didn't end up on my back.

However, when my foot went through the guy, I got to read all of his thoughts.

All of what he was about to do to me.

So I closed my eyes and went inside the scum. Now I knew for a fact I was in a cesspool, swimming in the shit that this guy called thoughts. If I got out of here I would need about ten showers.

If ghosts took showers.

As he reached for my right breast, I shouted at the top of my lungs, "No!"

And trust me, I can be loud.

Just ask anyone who sat beside me at a Broncos' football game.

And I was inside the guy when I shouted.

Slime-bucket grabbed his head and rolled over backward, the intense pain striking everywhere.

As he rolled away, I managed to stand my ground and get out of his body. I shook myself, wishing I could forget the memories of what I had just seen in his mind.

It would take twenty showers before I would feel clean again.

The guy was holding his head and screaming and rolling on the ground. Blood was coming out of his ears.

Both ears.

"Wow, what did you do to him?" a voice behind me asked.

I turned around to see a handsome couple standing to one side looking shocked. Both were about my height of five-ten, both wore jeans, expensive shirts, and tennis shoes.

"The pervert was about to get his jollies on my dead body, so I climbed inside his head and shouted as loud as I could."

Both of them laughed.

Then the woman stepped forward. "I'm Jewel and this is Tommy. We came to help get you used to being a ghost, but guess you are doing just fine."

I shook both their hands, happy as hell I had company.

"I'm Marble Grant. And got a hunch I'm going to need a lot of help."

"Someone close to you?" Tommy asked, pointing at Handsome Bob.

"Knew him for thirty minutes," I said. "Blind date. But I had planned on getting much closer to him after dinner, if you get my drift."

Jewel laughed and Tommy actually blushed a little, which I loved. I had a feeling I was going to like these two.

"I suppose you two are Ghost Agents. Right?"

Both of them looked shocked.

"I was a superhero in the hospitality and real estate side of the world," I said. "Any chance you two know Patty Ledgerwood and Poker Boy?"

"We do," Jewel said.

"You know," I said, "I'm damn hungry and I assume there is a way ghosts eat, so any chance we could get out of this smell and grab a bite and you guys call Patty and have her meet us. I would kind of like to tell her about my sudden death myself, since she has been my best friend for a hundred years now, give or take."

Both of them just nodded.

"Anything we need to do with that guy?" I asked, looking down at the scum who had killed me and Handsome Bob before I had the chance to find out if the handsome part went all the way to Bob's southern regions.

Greasy hair was still rolling on the dirty concrete, holding his ears and screaming. He was losing a lot of blood through his fingers. I clearly had done some damage.

"I think he's finished," Tommy said, laughing.

"Yeah," Jewel said. "Got to remember that trick."

With that we jumped to a place I knew well and loved, the Golden Nugget Buffet in downtown Las Vegas.

Now I knew I was really going to like these two.

CHAPTER THREE

The Golden Nugget Buffet had been decorated in all warm brown cloth and polished brass. Plants ringed the outside of the side part of the dining room nearest the escalator and the tables were solid, as were the chairs.

My hand went right through a chair as I tried to pull it out and Jewel did it for me.

"You'll learn how to actually move some physical matter, but you don't want to do that too often because people start to get spooked."

"I'll bet," I said.

Tommy jumped away to find Patty, and Jewel led me up to the wonderful smelling food. The images from the murderer's head were slowly fading, something I was very grateful for.

"Be careful to not run into anyone," Jewel said, indicating the six people around the large buffet area. "You end up reading their thoughts."

"Yeah, learned that with the guy who shot me," I said.

Jewel showed me how to pick up a plate, which was actually just the ghost component of the plate, and how to take food from the buffet.

In five minutes of filling a ghost plate with ghost food, I managed to not run into anyone alive, which sort of felt like a victory. I called it the dance of the living. A living person came toward me, I stepped sideways and went around them.

Jewel did the same, seemingly without noticing.

Back at the table, I bit into a piece of prime rib and damn near had an orgasm right there at the table.

Jewel just smiled as I moaned and kept on eating the fantastic tasting food.

"I remember the food being good here," I said after a few bites, "but never this good."

"Everything is better when you are a ghost," Jewel said. "Food tastes better, emotions are more powerful, and the travel and living is easier."

"Sex?" I asked.

"As the joke goes," Jewel said, smiling, "it's to die for."

"Oh, no," I said. "I had enough trouble controlling myself when I was alive."

Jewel just laughed and at that moment Tommy appeared.

"Patty is in Poker Boy's office," Tommy said. "Let's just

grab some food and jump there. She's expecting us but doesn't know why yet."

It dawned on me why Patty couldn't jump here. She was still alive. Anyone in the restaurant would see her arrive and then talk to no one. Not a good idea.

Tommy headed for the buffet. I really needed to pee, but instead I kept eating as we waited for him. Damn, the food was so good. I was going to be lucky to not gain a ton of weight now that I had died. I needed to remember to ask Jewel and Tommy how they stayed so thin.

After Tommy came back with a full plate of food, he jumped the three of us and our food and drink to what I assumed was Poker Boy's office, although I had never been there.

In fact, the place was like a legend.

But I had heard it was something special and I had heard right. The office wasn't really an office. It was more like a tile platform floating in the air a thousand feet over the Strip.

All four walls were freaking clear glass with a wood railing about waist high all the way around.

Without that railing, I would have been so afraid of falling off that slick checkered tile floor, I would have been clinging to the furniture and screaming like a ten-year-old girl not wanting to go see her uncle.

And I was dead, so pretty certain the fall wouldn't kill me again.

Still, scary damn place and now I really had to pee.

I made my heart stop racing and looked around.

In the very center of the room was this huge 1950s style diner booth, with a scarred tabletop and red vinyl booth seats on three sides. The thing was big enough to hold ten people if the people really liked each other.

There were half-a-dozen chairs around the room that could be pulled up to the open end of the booth I suppose, but three of them just sat facing out over the incredible view of the city.

And wow, what a view. I had always loved the lights of Las Vegas. Just never seen them from the air like this before.

"Marble," Patty said as we appeared. "Tommy said you needed to talk with me. Everything all right? You could have just called you know?"

"Not sure I knew how exactly," I said, smiling at my best friend.

Jewel laughed as she set her food and mine on the booth table.

Patty was wearing her MGM Grand Front Desk uniform of dark slacks, tan blouse and a lighter tan vest. She had her long hair pulled back and was as stunning as ever.

Patty frowned, something I had rarely seen her do in a century.

I glanced at my food on the booth table, then turned back to my friend. "Got myself killed while on a blind date about thirty minutes ago."

Patty's eyes went totally round. "Are you all right?"

"Pretty sure I'm dead," I said, laughing. I pointed to my forehead. "Bullet right there did the trick."

Patty looked like she was about to cry.

"Can I hug her?" I asked, glancing back at Jewel.

"She's a superhero," Jewel said, "and she can see you, so sure, don't know why not?"

I stepped toward Patty and she hugged me so hard, I wasn't sure I would be able to breathe.

And I hugged her back.

I guess, for the first time, it was sinking in that I had really died.

I was still here but I was dead.

That just sucked.

Except for the part about the food tasting so much better.

FINISH READING
BEING DEAD (THE FIRST YEAR): A MARBLE GRANT NOVEL

Get More Marble Grant

DeanWesleySmithStore.com

Hear From Dean

Want More From Dean?

For Dean Wesley Smith's newsletter
go to deanwesleysmith.com.

Get the latest news and releases from all of WMG's authors and lines, including Kristine Grayson, Kris Nelscott, *Pulphouse Magazine*, and so much more...

To sign up, **go to wmgbooks.com.**

About the Author
Dean Wesley Smith

Considered one of the most prolific writers working in modern fiction, *New York Times* and *USA Today* bestselling writer, Dean Wesley Smith published over two hundred novels and over seven hundred books in forty years, and hundreds and hundreds of short stories. He has over thirty million copies of his books in print.

At the moment he produces novels in four major series, including the time travel **Thunder Mountain** novels set in the old west, the galaxy-spanning **Seeders Universe** series, the cold case mystery series, **Cold Poker Gang** series, and the superhero series staring **Poker Boy.**

During his career, Dean also wrote a couple dozen *Star Trek* novels, the only two original *Men in Black* novels, Spider-Man and X-Men novels, plus novels set in gaming and television worlds. Writing with his wife Kristine Kathryn Rusch under the name Kathryn Wesley, they wrote the novel for the NBC miniseries **The Tenth Kingdom** and other books for *Hallmark Hall of Fame* movies.

He wrote novels under dozens of pen names in the worlds

of comic books and movies, including novelizations of almost a dozen films, from *X-Men* to *The Final Fantasy* to *Steel* to *Rundown*.

Dean also worked as a fiction editor off and on, starting at Pulphouse Publishing, then at *VB Tech Journal*, then Pocket Books, and now at WMG Publishing where he and Kristine Kathryn Rusch serve as executive editors for the acclaimed *Fiction River* anthology series. He took over the editorship of the acclaimed *Pulphouse Magazine* in 2018.

For more information about Dean's books and ongoing projects, please visit his website at www.deanwesleysmith.com

facebook.com/deanwsmith3

patreon.com/deanwesleysmith

bookbub.com/authors/dean-wesley-smith